COMRADE PAPA

GauZ'

COMRADE PAPA

Translated from the French by
Frank Wynne

BIBLIOASIS
Windsor, Ontario

First published in French as *Camarade Papa* by Le Nouvel Attila, Paris, in 2018

First published in North America in 2024 by Biblioasis

FIRST EDITION
1   3   5   7   9   10   8   6   4   2

Library and Archives Canada Cataloguing in Publication
Title: Comrade Papa / Gauz' ; translated from the French by Frank Wynne.
Other titles: Camarade papa. English
Names: Gauz, 1971- author. | Wynne, Frank, translator.
Series: Biblioasis international translation series ; 49.
Description: Series statement: Biblioasis international translation
series ; 49 | Translation of: Camarade papa.
Identifiers: Canadiana (print) 20240375335 | Canadiana (ebook) 20240375343
ISBN 9781771966450 (softcover) | ISBN 9781771966467 (EPUB)
Subjects: LCGFT: Novels.
Classification: LCC PQ3989.3.G38 C3613 2024 | DDC 843/.92—dc23

ROYAUME-UNI

This book is supported by the Institut français
(Royaume-Uni) as part of the Burgess programme.

Readied for the press by Daniel Wells
Designed and typeset in Nocturne by Patty Rennie
Cover designed by Nathan Burton

PRINTED AND BOUND IN CANADA

For Lounès, Aléki, L'Anges et les Visiteurs
History, a lie of no-one's choosing
At best, a tale made more amusing
Of an era and its musings

To René Ménil
born Negro, died communist

CONTENTS

BRIEF NOTE

The presence of the French in Côte d'Ivoire dates back to the mid-seventeenth century and greatly increased with the establishment of a number of colonial trading posts. This hindrance to British control of the Gulf of Guinea provoked tensions between the two countries. When French forces were repatriated after the country's devastating defeat in the Battle of Sedan, a small number of trading houses found that they were the sole defenders of the Tricolour against the British and the local tribes. These companies occupied a narrow strip of coastline: contemporary maps of the country were almost entirely blank.

Arthur Verdier, a businessman from La Rochelle, who served as resident of the establishment of "Côte d'Ivoire" from 1871 to 1889, had ambitions to create a private mining concession. His agent, Marcel Treich-Laplène, oversaw exploratory missions and signed agreements with local chieftains. But it was a military officer, Louis-Gustave Binger, who, having rallied support from Dakar (in Senegal) to Kong (in the far north of Côte d'Ivoire), had the glory of establishing the borders of the country and being appointed its first governor. The colony officially came into existence on March 10, 1893. In the same year, Verdier's businesses in Grand-Bassam were swept away by a tidal wave, which neatly coincides with this rewriting of history.

The Shoreline

Seven rolling breakers, their crests whipped by the wind, foam with rage as they pound their heads onto the beach. As the first wave shatters, spreading its halo over the golden sands, out at sea a second rears its head in a roar as thunderous as that which came before. Theirs is a short lifespan. As the remains of the first begins to ebb, the second surges forward, about to break. Ebb and flow shatter as they clash and retreat towards the deep. As four waves push from behind, and two beat a retreat into its belly, the third wave swells, billows, bellows louder than the last. The tip of the crest – they call it the "mother" – soars high above the others.

The arithmetic of this wave is unalterable. The first white sailors called it the "Rip of Guinea". It is conceived above the Devil's Well, an abyssal fault created by the contractions of the nascent earth's crust. To approach it is perilous, to brave it, impossible. No man has ever come by sea to settle these lands. Safe anchorage is possible only four hundred metres from land. Men and merchandise are moved from ship to land in sturdy dugout boats, whalers paddled by the only two peoples in the world who can defy the rip tide: the Nzema and the Kru.

In creating the rip tide, nature elected to offer a mite of balance to relations between the white and the Black peoples. Ships that were marooned, in peril, or simply anchored out at sea, wishing to trade with the indigenous peoples, would run up a flag. White for the Francays, because of their taste for ivory. Red for the Anglays, great traders in rifles and gunpowder. Black for the Portugays, inveterate traffickers in "ebony" – slaves to be shipped to the four corners of the known world. But, regardless of nationality, the ship's captain gives "the Sign". He climbs down into a lifeboat, places one foot on the gunwale, and, holding on to the edge, plunges his index and middle fingers into the sea and brings them up to his eyes: "I would rather go blind than go back on my word." The market is open. The dugouts are launched!

Every month, a steamship from the Compagnie des Chargeurs Réunis, S.A. (head office: 1, boulevard Malesherbes, 75008 Paris) leaves Le Havre for our colonies in Cochinchina, by way of the Cape of Good Hope. After brief layovers at La Rochelle and Bordeaux, which are the lifeblood of the slave trade, it makes a series of short hops, stopping at the colonial trading posts that encircle the fat proboscis of West Africa: the Canary Islands, Saint-Louis, Dakar, Conakry, Monrovia, Cape Palmas, Béréby, Lahou and Grand-Bassam. Skirting the coastline is a legacy of the era of sailing ships, when people imagined that fierce westerly winds led to the foothills of hell. Agents, customs officers, clerks, bureaucrats and army rabble...anyone and everyone being posted to the colonies arrives aboard one of the Chargeurs' ships. To reach Grand-Bassam takes sixteen days. At this point, everyone on the shore knows that a ship belching black smoke *is about to appear on the horizon on the other side of the rip tide.*

On the beach, there are a dozen civil servants and factors from the trading post – almost the entire white population. Each is flanked by a "boy" whose duty, at this moment, is to rectify any physiological injustice. Against the sun, melanin for the Black "boy"; for the white man, a parasol held by the "boy". Also present are Mandé-Dyula porters, Senegalese infantrymen, groups of Aboureys, Akapless rebels. The Nzema rowers odiously prolong their night, lying in the star-spangled shade of phototropic coconut palms that curl their long necks towards the waves. Of the Kru, who are even more phlegmatic than their rivals, there is little sign. The ethnology of Grand-Bassam is complete.

On this morning, September 5, 1893, the beach is more crowded than usual. Bodies and minds are drawn to a new issue. For some months now, this shoreline has been French, and with it everything that lives and breathes as far as the Tenth Parallel, more than six hundred kilometres north of here. It is official: the first governor of Côte d'Ivoire is arriving aboard the Capitaine Ménard. *For years now, it has been accepted wisdom that, while whips and bullets can subjugate, symbols alone can truly conquer. Of these, the most important is the grand arrival. This has been carefully crafted. We are not about to repeat the mistakes of History. Today, the rip tide will be with us.*

On the port side, the first skiff to bob to the rhythm of the current is Nzema. A windlass lowers a net containing several crates. When the first Kru dugout comes alongside, a white man appears, shipshape from cap to boots. He is lowered into the whaling boat. He stands ramrod straight. From the shore, he looks like a man walking upon the waters. He plunges his index and middle fingers into the swell and brings them up to his eyes. The sign, long since fallen into disuse, is instantly recognised by all. As the Kru push off, they launch into a song no-one has ever heard. The four bars of this mysterious chant are carried on the wind to the shore: "Abreuhhhh vehno syonnnn..." The crowd begins to roar. The Senegalese infantrymen, recognising the anthem, get to their feet and, Chassepots at their shoulders, they run to form two lines. "Abreuhhhh vehno syonnnn..." The last line of the Marseillaise, with Kru words and accents, da capo al coda.

The skiff is well suited to its English name, "surfboat". It skims over mother ocean. The seven paddles are brandished towards the heavens, the white man stands erect, holding the Tricolour at arm's length, expression haughty, chin high. A few deft manoeuvres by the helmsman, and the skiff comes to a standstill facing the Senegalese infantrymen's guard of honour. Shouts and cheers. Louis-Gustave Binger, former infantry captain, former explorer of the River Niger, first governor of Côte d'Ivoire, comes ashore in Grand-Bassam. Behold as French officialdom debarks in its colony.

A RED FLAG CHAPTER

The RAAC

Days, weeks, I don't know when Maman left. I take a book from her desk. Comrade Papa turns off the lights, in a hurry to get going. He doesn't say anything. He never says anything. Unless it's about the struggle for the emancipation of the working masses. We go down the stairs. We live on Sintannenstraat – the street of Saint Anne, mother of the Virgin Mary. By the mouth of the building are the men from Marie-Anna's gang. The suppositories of the capitalist system. The police, a reactionary force of lackeys in the pay of the bourgeoisie, don't do anything, because this is a working-class district. Warmoesstraat, we turn right. My proletarian primary school is on this street. It's also the street where women sell smooches. While we are learning history, they're practising the world's oldest profession, in the city's oldest district.

I was born here. I know every window, and all the girls know me. On our working-class class outings, I *goedendag* everyone. Moody Marko hisses, "*Klootzak.*" Result: class warfare and hair-pulling. We end up on the ground in a tangle of limbs. The other kids in our working-class class scream and

9

laugh, the teachers tear their hair out, Yolanda comes and pulls Marko off me. The class war always starts outside Yolanda's window. Marko is wrong: Maman doesn't sell kisses. Comrade Papa says Maman's just a Miss Guided socialist.

Yolanda's skin is dark brown, like Comrade Papa's. Maman's light brown, like mine. Yolanda says we're the Maroon tribe. She's the only Maroon who sells kisses on our street. After every class war, she gives me a public ticking off. On account of how eyes are prejudiced when it comes to colour, so Maroons have to be exemplary. It's the burden of the Maroons. When it's just the two of us, she says: "You're very brave." All I know is that littler kids have to fight to seize class privileges from bigger kids. And Moody Marko is the biggest kid in the working-class class . . .

The day Comrade Papa and I are set to leave, we walk past Yolanda's window. I make our secret sign; she looks the other way. Yolanda always looks the other way when I make her sad. Like the time I went missing and parked up at Amsterdam Centraal station. When Yolanda comes round to put me down when Comrade Papa's out militating revolutionary China somewhere and Maman's at the big library studying Albanianism, we have Big-Yolanda-Nights. But that night, I insubordinated Party discipline. Yolanda searched everywhere for me. Just when she was about to drop dead from all the fears and worries in her tummy, I came back like a boomerang. When she pressed me to her big nooky pillows, I heard her heart beating the boom-boom of the Boni-Marrons. I told her I'd gone missing so I could park up to look at the big clock

10

and the trains. That it's not fair, being born next to a train station and never getting to see real live trains on account of Party
discipline. That over the loudspeakers at the station, I heard
the voice of the She-Devil, a smooch-seller who's as old as the
red-light district. Yolanda grinned her big white teeth. I swore
on the picture of Comrade Mao that hangs over my bed that I
wouldn't go missing again without telling her first.

Yolanda made me sad when she looked the other way the
day of my first expedition. Papa and me are at the Oude Kerk,
the local parish, when Yolanda screams after me. Still wearing
her nooky uniform, she runs down the street. The law says
working girls aren't allowed to be streetworkers in the street,
only in their windows. Especially not outside the church
where they used to bury poor dead people. People's eyes are
already filled with prejudices about women and Maroons.
So what will they think about a woman who's a Maroon and
a smooch-seller all in the same body? She has absolutely
no respect for Party discipline, my Yolanda. To make things
worse, there could be reactionary forces lurking, just waiting
to issue fines and score penalties and ruin days of hard graft
selling smooches.

As she runs, her spiky shoes and her big bazoomas
dance the glories of the working people, the best dance of
all. With a swipe, Yolanda sickles me off the ground. It's not
just her heart beating the boom-boom of the Boni-Marrons,
she's blubbing like a baby. She doesn't have to. I'm not going
to go missing and park up at Amsterdam Centraal like last
time, I'm with Comrade Papa. She hugs me hard against her
gentlemen's all-sorts. She hammers me onto the ground and

11

stuffs a huge bag of kids' all-sorts – liquorice, my favourites. Yolanda is magic. But I'm a revolutionary solider of the sovereign people arising, so I can't even be corrupticated by my favourite sweets. I give Yolanda a ticking off. She stops crying and ends up grinning her big teeth at my revolutionary stands. She promises me she won't do it again. I give her a look with my commissioner of propaganda eyes, the Yan'an Rectification eyes that can spot a Lin Biao. I feel reassured. I look at her with my Boni-Marron eyes from the forests of Suriname. We make our secret sign. She walks away. Outside the Oude Kerk, I'm not the only one watching her walk away. She turns back once and makes our secret sign twice. Once for her, once for me. From behind the wall of my mouth, I shout: "Vaarwel, Yolanda!"

At the far end of Warmoesstraat, the final frontier of the district, we duck and dive into a little alley, so as to avoid the Damrak, the roadblock, and run slap bang into Prins Hendrikkade. Comrade Papa doesn't forget to rant and rave something against all the royal families in the world. I'm not listening, I'm too excited. At the other end of the street is Amsterdam Centraal. The big clock says 9.04. Amsterdam to Paris departing at 9.58, says the She-Devil in the loudspeakers. First journey. First on the train. Comrade Papa is carrying my foreign affairs case. In my rucksack, I've put the same things I take with me to working-class class: books. Yolanda's all-sorts are in there too. Before boarding, Comrade Papa tells me that Maman has left to go to the socialist paradise of Comrade Hodja, the man in the clouds on the poster over her desk. She doesn't want to have regrets like she did last year when

12

Comrade Mao died. Besides, Amédée Pierre's band needs her tactical support. She didn't have time to anticipate. Socialist necessity.

Comrade Papa didn't have to put on his serious face to get me aboard. I'm really happy to be taking the train for the first time with Comrade Papa. Not only that – we're heading to the Paris Commune. No steam, no whistles, the train moves off without any noise because of the electrical current. I lean out the window. I imagine the crowd on the platform waving white handkerchiefs at me. The Great Helmsman if he's oriental, the Little Father of the Peoples if he's accidental, sets off, carrying the torch of truth to some future revolution. There's a lot of commotion in Amsterdam Centraal, but it's not popular fervour. The yolk of capitalism brings down the masses. Luckily, Comrade Papa is going to have a revolution and the people will rise up and be The People, and they'll have smiles like you see on the posters from the People's Republic of China and the Supreme Soviet blu-tacked on my bedroom walls. The train pulls out without worrying what I'm thinking, without a smile from anyone in the station but me.

In the carriage, Comrade Papa talks loudly. No-one complains. People will put up with diatribes in languages they don't understand. At home, Maman talks to me in school Dutch, and Comrade Papa in communist French. When they talk to each other, they cry. The cry of the sovereign people denouncing the evil capitalist control of means and resources. There are other kinds of cries that I don't understand. But the cry of the sovereign people between Maman and Comrade Papa is something I like hearing. At least then they're with me.

13

I'll be spending a lot of time with Comrade Papa on the train journey so I'm happy and a half!

On Big-Maman-Nights, she scribbles notes in the pile of books on her desk. I pretend I'm like her, making notes in books from school and from the library. The longer I spend noting books, the longer I get to stay with Maman, so I write notes and notes. And if I can note long enough, Maman eventually stops her notes. She gets up and she puts her arms around me. Maman says that the stories that really move us have to be locked deep in our hearts so we don't forget. So on Big-Maman-Nights we have prisoner swaps: my stories from the working-class classroom, including my fights with Moody Marko, in exchange for her dreams of socialist Africa. She also tells me tales of agrarian forms in Albania and in proper Korea, the northern one, not the evil capitalist one. I don't always understand Maman's prisoners. But she uses such beautiful amazing words. As for my prisoners, I draw and quarter them, I rack them and pinion them, and when they're all gone, I tell them all over again with special made-up words so Maman will think they're beautiful. I stay with her for as long as my words and my body can stay awake. When I'm on the edge of sleep, she hums me a song by the Amédée Pierre gang.

On mornings after Big-Maman-Nights, I catch up on sleep in working-class class. The teachers don't disturb me. I'm loads of lessons ahead of everyone else. Actually, my teachers say I'm years ahead of myself. They want me to go to a special school a long way from our neighbourhood. Sacriprivilege! We live in the red quarter. The most beautiful area of the city. Comrade

Papa cat-and-gorically refuses to let me leave the working-class class, because a true revolutionary should never be cut off from the lumpy proletariat. That's how they make consumer capitalists. I'm ashamed of being years ahead of myself. I don't want to be a rabid dog of the ruling class barking at workers and stockpiling extra years and not sharing them with the labouring classes.

On Big-Comrade-Papa-Nights, everything is a weapon in the struggle against blind stateless big capitalism. The whole place is a Revolutionary Anti-Capitalist Camp – we call it the RACC. The fridge is the extra surplus-value; the shelves of pasta and tinned food are the concrete capital; the broom is an AK47; the vacuum cleaner is a Zhukov T-series tank; the bathroom is the Strategic Command Centre HQ; the toilet is the fallback position or, if I don't behave, it's a re-education camp.

The menu is a five-year-plan that lasts four days. I'm always a minister, but my title changes depending on what I'm doing. Minister of Aquatic and Bath-Related Affairs, Minister of Education and School Supplies, Minister of Poetry and Piano Practice, Minister of the War on Cockroaches and Toilet Paper, Minister in Control of Cooking Pasta and Rice, Minister of Short- and Long-Wave Radio . . . When we were developing the RACC, I was every single minister. Well, all except Minister for Propaganda, Historical Perspective and Dialectical Materials. Those were reserved for Comrade Papa. The sincere joy of the working masses, the relentless class struggle without so much as a please or thank you and the sacred union of the working classes, the Comintern, the oh, pressed people, the wonky non-aligned countries, the unconscionable colonies of Africa and Asia . . . Comrade Papa has lots of lovely phrases, and he never talks down to me, he speechifies. Our official ideology is the New Commune. On days when his face is all tired and lined because his brain is full to bursting with the final struggle of peoples against the capitalist monster, he gets lost and he stops right in the middle of his revolutionary speechifying. He looks at me and in his eyes I see pity or maybe embarrassment. I don't like it when that happens. I don't want to disappoint him, so I militate with every bone in my revolutionary soul. Raised fist, outstretched arm, victory sign, open hands, steely stare, survey the horizon, I repeat these over and over in front of the mirror or to Yolanda. She doesn't understand communistic French, but she grins with all her teeth and she looks at me with something like pity or maybe embarrassment . . .

On Big-Yolanda-Nights, Yolanda arrives all dressed up and even prettier than in the uniform she wears for selling kisses. She brings colour, and not just on account of her clothes, but because she talks about Blacks and whites and Boni-Marrons. Her country, Suriname, in America where the Indians live, is full of Boni-Marrons from Black Africa. They went there by force, on account of slave work, which is different from the work of the working classes because you work and you don't get paid. A Marxist-Leninist contradiction, says Comrade Papa, since all work is deserving of renumeration.

Slave work only exists in the mind of the slaver, because, inside his head, a slave is always free. That's what makes him a Boni-Marron, according to Yolanda. At the first opportunity, *zoom*, he escapes into the jungle. Marrons know the jungles of Indian America as well as the forest they left behind in the Black Africa of Maman and Comrade Papa. Yolanda's Boni-Marrons are a tribe of Blacks who escaped the slavery plantations for the forests. She doesn't like it when I ask her questions about slave work. She prefers to tell me stories about kids from her tribe of Boni-Marrons in the green jungles. She uses lots of words we don't get taught at school. They dance on her tongue, skate across her teeth and spill from her lips. She tells stories with lots of laughs. Yolanda's mouth is pretty when she laughs.

When it's time for bed I play at being a little kid because she likes that. She sits on the edge of my bed and takes up all the room. When she sings songs of the Boni-Marrons from the green forest, I can't understand her words, but I can still hear her heart, because her gentlemen's all-sorts are right next to my face. With all the kisses she has to sell, Yolanda is a lot more tired than me. So on nights when she doesn't do her smooch-selling, she needs to rest. I yawn and then close my eyes so she thinks I'm asleep. Before she goes home, or heads back to her window for men to stare at, we make our secret sign. With her right thumb folded against her palm, she presses her four splayed fingers against my heart and then against her own heart. When she does it, one of her gentlemen's all-sorts tries to escape from her flowery blouse. Now it's my turn to make the sign on her heart then on my heart.

When Ogun forges men from iron and tender clay, they have four fingers on each hand. One day, a fifth grows away from all the others. The fifth allows men to do many things they can't do with the original four. The lives of men are changed. But progress brings good things and bad stuff in the same sack. Wickedness and selfishness come with the fifth finger. Humanity is divided, men tear each other apart, they lose the memory of past happiness. But out in the green jungle, Yolanda's tribe of Boni-Marrons in Suriname still remember that man was forged from iron and tender clay with four equal fingers. They make our secret sign so that they never forget.

A ROMAN CHAPTER

Dabilly

Because of how my name is spelled, the nationality of "i"s is the first thing that intrigues me when I start school. "There is the Roman 'i' and the Greek 'i', that's just the way things are. Now stop asking foolish questions and concentrate on your lessons," barks the schoolmaster. "The twin branches of the Greek 'y' embody a whole culture. The Romans brought them together to make a universal 'i'. The dot on top of the 'i' is the true beginning of civilisation," explains Father, re-explaining after his fashion. The distance between school and our house is more than physical.

In the mornings, I walk with Maman. We stray from the road and wander through the "gallery"; this dense tunnel of vegetation that runs along the banks of the Claise is what gave our house its name: La Galerette. In winter, it is warmer, in summer, cooler. Mother speaks little. As do I. We tread on our own thoughts. In the treetops, the ballet of squirrels; in the brush, the dance of the foxes; in the air, the thrum of the insects and the song of the birds. My favourite is the king-fisher. The name, the blue plume, the mechanical call like the sounds from the smeltery along our route. They say that in Châtellerault, at the "end of the world", there is an even bigger smelt works.

As you arrive in Abilly, the River Claise divides to form a "y", and we follow the right fork. Seen from the stone bridges, the silver birches descend in serried ranks along the bridle path to the artificial waterfall created to give an impetus to the water as it hurls itself into the mill wheel at Rives. The Conty dynasty have converted an ancient convent into the largest flour mill in the region. In the capitulum where novitiates once read the martyrology, millstones turned by hydraulic force crush the wheat, thereby liberating fine particles that are flammable and toxic to the bronchial tubes. Mother works there and stays there. I continue my schooling, behind the church dedicated to Saint Martin, my favourite saint.

Father left his country at a young age. They say he travelled all the way to Paris. He came home when Grandfather died. With him came the "foreigner", already with child, which means that I was conceived in a state of sin. It is possible that I am not Father's child. My red curls are very different from his thick black hair. Her eyes, too blue for such dark locks, her skin so pale, Mother looks like all the strumpets who work in the Paris dance halls. Here in the village, I have been reminded of this litany of sins ever since I could string two words together. I was born and grew up in Abilly, a town whose name is inscribed on my birth certificate, yet I do not feel at home here. I have always dreamed of leaving. At catechism class, where I am most assiduous, I have learned that the redemption of the soul comes through departure.

Alone, or with an entire people; from Genesis to the Book of Revelation, people leave in order to be free, in order to fulfil their fate.

On Sundays, I serve at Mass. For a brief moment, I am an altar boy rather than the son of a stranger and a foreigner. Father Mathieu shows me off. I am regularly called to recite whole epistles before his flock. In truth, my Latin is very basic. Though precise when I begin my prayers, I gradually introduce scraps and later whole passages that have little to do with the tongue of Caesar. The fact remains that I have an excellent memory, and an ear for the music of the language. One evening, I confessed to the prelate.

"*Pater meus, chlamydem opto cadere et animas amissas tegere . . . tamquam sanctum Martinen.*"

Father Mathieu weeps for joy. Together we kneel. He sees in this the plan of the Almighty; I see it as an escape. A letter from him and I find myself accepted at the seminary in Tours . . . *tamquam sanctum Martinen*, like Saint Martin.

* * *

Several years of mortification, prayers and classes in real Latin have kept me cloistered in search of Discernment. I have never set foot outside the bishopric. When Mother is dying, I am granted a leave of absence. I return to Abilly. On the outskirts of the village, I take the path through the "gallery", our path. It seems barely recognisable. The trees are shrunken, there are no squirrels, no kingfishers, no foxes now, the Claise looks more like a stream than a river. I find my mother confined to bed. Her skin is paler than I remember. Her blue eyes twinkle when she sees me. She is still beautiful, even when she coughs up clouds of flour and spits gobs of plaster. Out in the fields, Father is gathering stones. Dozens of them. Cut, chiselled, polished flints . . . He harvests them from earth freshly tilled by the plough and carefully stores them in what he calls his "reliquary", a trunk next to the hearth. He speaks to his stones with the gravity of a senator. Adopting various voices, he re-creates their conversations. At first, people laugh; they assume that he is soused. But the scenes are long and involve a complex dramaturgy. Madness? The neighbours believe so. Personally, I doubt it. Spouting nonsense is not an illness, else half the village would be locked up. Besides, an asylum is no place for a man who, out in his field, works harder than the pair of oxen that drive his plough.

Proselytiser, preceptor, oracle, soothsayer, high priest, legionnaire, senator . . . Mother recognises the characters he inhabits. She identifies them, gives them names, knows how to answer them, to anticipate their words, assuage their fears, temper their passions. The state of Mother is not alien to the state of Father, and vice versa. One evening, Mother goes to bed and gutters out. A candle snuffed, a wisp of blue smoke, then nothing but a mass of wax. She is interred the following morning.

I do not have the strength to immediately return to my apostolic studies. Mother dead, Father founders. Gradually, the Roman becomes his central character. His lands become empire, the cart a chariot, the cattle chargers, the calls of *hup!* the cries of gladiators. Whether standing sentry at the entrance to his field, or lying in ambush behind a drystone wall, he is always armed with a pilum and a shield and a pewter pot by way of a helmet.

One morning, after sentry duty, the Roman strides towards me, tremulous and menacing. I fear that he will call me a Gaul. Before he collapses, I hear him whisper: "*Tu quoque fili.*" Finally, I can put him to bed. Four hours later, as I dab a flannel on his brow, he jolts awake, eyes starting from their sockets, radiating heat. My attention is caught by a trickle of snot flecked with brownish clots dripping from his left nostril.

"The land belongs to us. We subjugated it. This is our home, Maximus, heed my words. It is we who gave them the language to discuss and appreciate wine. It is to us these Gauls owe their civilisation. I have ploughed the furrows. You need only follow them, my dear Maximus. If I should fall upon the field of battle, take my shield, my pilum and my stones. Forget not the reliquary. Swear that you will take the reliquary. It houses the voices of our ancestors. The stones . . ."

I sneeze. A reflexive salvo. The force of the blast sets damp strands of hair fluttering about Father's brow and he falls silent. He is as surprised as I. As my mouth half opens and my nose twitches, he fears a second salvo. Then his face relaxes. He lets go of me, sinks back into the sweat-damp sheets. I sneeze a second time. In the self-same bed as Mother, Father dies in the role of Abilius, the Roman legionnaire who founded the city of Abilly.

* * *

Three weeks, two burials and a lineage that comes down to me alone. Now sole proprietor of La Galerette, I feel as though I never left. The earth anchors bodies and souls. Should they not see me again, the congregation will dispatch a priest. He will find the house boarded up. The thought comes to me as I listen to a kingfisher whose call echoes the steam-driven pistons of the foundry. I wish to go to Châtellerault, "the ends of the earth" of my childhood. I slide the key beneath a flint carved and polished by who knows what hands in the distant past, one that Father did not have time to put away.

The Claise and I, we flow due west, towards Creuse. My own shadow trailing after me makes me feel that I am being followed by Father, by his monologues obsessed with civilisation. In the middle of the farmyard, he would restage scenes from the Assemblée Nationale: Ferry by the pigsty, Clemenceau by the chicken coop.

His acting is extravagant. He leaps when there are cheers, shakes a vengeful fist when there are boos. In the Palais Bourbon, the honourable Jules Ferry struts like a cockerel towards the dais:

"I repeat that there is a right for the superior races, because there is a duty for them. They have the duty to civilise the inferior races."

From the back of the benches to the right, Georges Clemenceau replies:

"Ever since I saw German scholars scientifically demonstrate that France had to be defeated because the Frenchman is of an inferior race, I confess, I think twice before declaring any man or civilisation inferior!"

Then, all of a sudden, the Roman in Father would appear. Take cover! Of course there are superior races! Why else would Roman send her legions into Gaul? Why else would France dispatch her legions to the *terra incognita Africae*? The debates in parliament today are little changed from those of the agora. My westward march transports my thoughts towards the Americas. How familiar do we find this young and distant continent, while our ancient neighbour, Africa, is still unknown.

* * *

Wheat, grapes, potatoes. The source of the Holy Trinity: bread, wine, soup ... When the countryside ceases to be a vast expanse of fields, a town is near. The roads are wider, and much busier. Infected by the bustle on the roads, I quicken my step. The waning day finds me at "the ends of the earth". Châtellerault. I ask directions from an elegant gentleman in a top hat, whose face is half hidden by a beard and banded by a moustache. With a pristine glove, he points the way to the rue Bourbon, and the rue Saint-Jacques. I lose my way. Another top-hat-beard-moustache-white-gloves sends me towards the Quai Napoléon 1er. When the street names alternate between canonised saints and French monarchs, the dwellings are opulent, the citizenry elegant, the carriages shiny. From the right bank, I see an arched stone bridge. Roman engineering: nine vaulted spans supporting a paved thoroughfare. I cross the river. To my right, a series of sawtooth roofs and twin red-brick towers: La Manufacture des Armes de Châtellerault. The famous munitions factory, known locally as the Manu, swallows and spits out the throng of *manusards*, the workers in their blue overalls and caps. The vast beating heart that powers the machines spews scalding water and boiling oils into the river and belches smoke and steam into the air. In the belly of the beast, there is light. For the first time, my dazzled eyes behold the miracle of the sprite that is electricity. As though to celebrate this genie, come the bells tolling vespers. A mere twenty kilometres, but, like Moses, Jesus and other embibled personages, I have walked... Should I carry on? Retrace my steps? Stop here? I know that Saint James stopped at Châtellerault on his great pilgrimage. Perhaps I too have made my first stop on the way to my own Compostela.

A CHAPTER ON GERMAN ALSACE

Of ARMAMENTS and BLOOSMUZIK

Châteauneuf is the name of the region on the far side of the bridge. An endless stream of horse-drawn carts, the streets smell of a mixture of manure and molten iron. Homes and workshops are stacked along the narrow thoroughfares. A far cry from the broad avenues and the soaring buildings on the far side of the river. No begloved bearded dandies in top hats, no elegant coaches, no mansions. In the span of a bridge, another world.

I follow the vesperal lament of the church tower. This will be my first Mass since the fatal sneeze. In the church-yard, there is a little chapel to the right-hand side of the main building. I slip inside, hoping to find some serenity of mind and some rest for my aching legs. It is full. Before I can turn back, the congregants in the last pew have shuffled over to make room for me. One finger in the murky waters of the font, a furtive sign of the cross, the stretch of pew is barely large enough to accommodate one buttock. My legs will not have their long-awaited rest. The Agnus Dei; the service is almost at an end. I wait for the customary *ritus conclusionis*, but lo, the priest begins to speak in German. He concludes the rite with an *auf Wiedersehen* that triggers a stampede for the doors. I am jostled and swept along by my liturgical benchmates. Outside, the throng is so dense one cannot help but wonder how so many found space in the tiny chapel. And, indeed, why they crammed inside when the nave of the main church is all but empty. The churchyard is filled with a cacophony of voices in the language of Goethe. I am utterly at sea, and this is evident. A man accosts me:

"You are not zo vell?"

"Excuse me?"

"You do not veelink zo gut?"

"Oh, no, I am fine. I did not quite understand you. Tell me, why does everyone here speak German?"

"German? Nein, ve do not schpeaken German here."

The man's reply is so categorical that I begin to doubt the language lessons I undertook to comprehend Bach and Haydn.

"I'm sorry, I thought that . . ."

"No need vor zorry. Vee are Alsatian here and we speakink Alsatian. Alzo, you do not say to other man he speakink German, he vill kill you perhaps."

" . . ."

"Do not vorry, I vill not to denounze you."

I must look thunderstruck. The man laughs and claps me on the back. I assume it is kindly meant.

"My name eet iz Pierre Munchène."

Handshake. Pierre is happy that I joined them in the little chapel rather than go into the large church with the "others". He talks fluently, despite flattening "f" to "v", lisping "s" to "z", exploding his "j" into "che", and ballooning his "p" into "b". Decrypting his speech in full flow requires something of a miracle. He pauses and asks me what I am doing; I tell him of my walk to the "ends of the earth", of my need to find food and lodging for the night. Without a moment's hesitation, he bids me follow him with a phrase that makes as much sense as concluding a Mass in German – excuse me, in Alsatian.

"Peoples vrom ze verkshops, vee are celebratink a new manacle. Come."

My first evening in Châteauneuf-près-Châtellerault is spent in a workman's shack that reeks of smoke, the smells of cooking and Alsatian labourers from the Manu.

In '70, after his disastrous defeat and capture at the Battle of Sedan, Napoleon III saved his imperial skin by suing for peace in abject surrender. Accordingly, in '71, to avoid the sight of Pickelhaube helmets marching down the Champs-Élysées, the French bourgeoisie ceded Alsace and part of Lorraine to the Prussian nobility. Overnight, the entire populace of Alsace found itself cut off from France, when, at the stroke of a pen, the region became the Imperial Territory of Alsace-Lorraine. To freely circulate, unmolested by the occupying troops, citizens are required to present an *Auswanderungsschien* – a permit to reside on their own lands. Given these conditions, many emigrated . . . to France. *Hallo*, Charleville, Saint-Étienne, Châtellerault. Many of them settle in the towns where munitions factories are being modernised, where their long-established skills in armaments are highly valued. There are so many Alsatians working at the Manu that, at times, Châteauneuf sounds like a market town deep in the country of storks. The little chapel I ventured into is dedicated to Saint Odile, patron saint of Alsace. But the officiating priest is freshly arrived from Diebling, a village in Moselle.

"How dare they send us a curate from Diebling! Those traitors from Moselle, sons of mercenaries, grandsons of hitmen, those men who speak German, dream of being German, are still considered French. And we're the ones being Germanised! Though this shame may last, still we shall have vengeance. Upon my word, one day Strasbourg shall be the capital of Europe."

This prediction comes from Pierre's best friend, Schäkele. We follow the path of the River Vienne. Pouring from the factory gates, Alsatians, in successive waves, have settled along the quays. A stone's throw from the cemetery, we have taken over a former cutlery works and transformed it into a tavern.

Sitting at a long table, I find it impossible to follow the countless Alsatian conversations. Pierre sits next to me and, despite his accent, serves as my interpreter. Around the great oak table, pitchers of wine waltz, making cheeks red and eyes bright. A shoulder of pork atop a bed of sauerkraut and new potatoes is passed from hand to hand. Between mouthfuls, Pierre talks about Stek, the arms inspector. An Alsatian of some note. People say he has the ear of Herr Treuille, the entrepreneur who, with the Conty brothers, is one of the chief investors in the Manu. Stek is behind the numerous *inchworms*. Labourers of unequal status rub shoulders in the arms factory: the "journeymen", employed for short periods or called in when there is a glut of work, and "mechanicals", who are guaranteed work and benefits for themselves and their families. The brass ring! Referring to them as 'manacles' is a little Alsatian joke.

Tonight, we raise a toast to Schäkele, the newest manacle. Forgers, welders, checkerers, riflers, pistol smiths, stockmakers, gun engravers – all here speak fluent MAC, the language of the Manufacture of Arms of Châtellerault. From their talk of firing pins, safety-catches, barrels, hammers, cocks, sights, springs, triggers, couplers, stops, breeches, chambers, one can learn all there is to know about rifles, from the Chassepot to the Gras to the Lebel. Mention of the handsomely named Lebel, the latest bolt-action infantry rifle to be made at the Manu, prompts a passionate polyphony of voices. The Lebel is beautiful, it is swift, it does not overheat, it does not jam, the Lebel is a repeating rifle, it is determined to kill. "If only we had had them at the battle of Sedan!" "That said, our Chassepots were better than their Dreyse needle-guns"; "'Twas the generals lost the battle for us"; "Our chance will come again, and we'll have our Lebels" ... The Alsatians of Châtellerault do more than simply make guns, they steel themselves for the fray.

The night draws on. We are the last stragglers in the pothouse. The table is strewn with the remnants of food. The ballet of wine jugs has slowed. The riflemen evoke the ills of the country. Or they talk of village fêtes to the rhythms of *bloosmuzik*, in which they bemoan their enforced exile, and conjure images of the kinsfolk they have left behind. In their nostalgia, the language is maternal. Schäkele takes it upon himself to rouse the table from its bilious humour. He launches an attack on Pierre.

"Ho, friend Peter, tell us a fine tale."

"Not B-eeter, dear Jacques, but B-ierre . . ."

General laughter. A personal surprise.

"His name is Peter, Peter Munchen. He has Frenchified his name as Pierre Munchène, yet of us all he is the only one with German blood. He was born there and raised among his mother's family. Who knows what brought him here? It is his fault that Guillaume sued for Alsace."

General laughter.

"Not again vill Alzass be Vrench. I am zaving time, Chaques, I am zaving time!"

Pierre or Peter is not disconcerted. He turns to me.

"Schäkele is Chaques. In schul, this already is how they call his leetle zon. In time ve vill all have Vrench names. Like the Generäle of Napoleon, zey are var behind ze times."

General laughter. Schäkele is actually Jacques, while Pierre is Peter; these German Alsatians, these French from Moselle, this Roman priest . . . this day signifies something. I needs must discover what. As though he can read my thoughts, Schäkele knows where I am bound. All those at the table join in the conversation.

"Some place where there is no talk of civilisation."

"Then you are bound for Africa."

"My leetle couzin is there now. His name iz Louis-Gustave. At home, ve zay LG."

"Where exactly is he?"

"He iz vrom Niederbronn, near Sarreguemines."

"Wo! Nicht wo*her*!"

"He asks where he *is*, not where he is *from*."

36

"*Kong,* they tell me, *Kong.*"

"The place is called the Congo."

"How zhould I know zees?"

"In Africa, there is the Congo and then Sudan. Nothing else."

"Zuudan, zis name I also know."

"As I thought. Your cousin has gone to the Congo in Sudan."

Comments come thick and fast. Conversations bifurcate at random. For the first time, I hear the name of Binger.

"Ven he leave here, he zwear to my Tante that he vill zurückkommen wiz land ten times as beeg as all Alzass and Lorraine."

"Nothing is bigger than Alsace and Lorraine."

"I zpeak of land."

"And where will he put this land of his?"

"In his pocket, by Jove."

"How so?"

"Two witnesses, an inkwell, a quill, some paper, an X signed in black and it is his!"

"He's right. The lands of Africa are naught but crosses on paper. The rules of ownership and the procedure for allotting them are but lately decided. And talk of procedure brings us back to Germany. Bismarck – may his pickelhaube be shoved up his arse – arranged it all in Berlin!"

"Those bastards with the needle-guns! They always get their way!"

"Who else was there?"

"All of Europe. Even the backward Belgians."

"They say a Britisher snatched the whole of the Congo from us."

"The Congo in the Sudan?"

"No, the Congo in the Congo."

"If the British have the Congo, what then have we?"

"The Congo is not British, it is Belgian."

"Zen why did zis man say ze British snatched it from us?"

"I didn't say the British, I said a Britisher. Stanley, the greatest explorer since Christopher Columbus. He gave the whole Congo to his benefactor, the king of the Belgians."

"They say this is where you find King Solomon's mines."

"King Solomon's mines are in Belgian hands?"

"O Zaint Odile, ze British should chop ze head ov zuch a traitor!"

"And you say these are the lands we lost?"

"No, no, we never lost them, since we never won them. We were too busy losing land back here in Europe."

"Solomon's mines or not, we have no business being in Negro lands when we cannot hold on to our own!"

"All our dead would not have died in vain if there were gold buried beneath our churches. In Africa, there is gold everywhere. We should go slaughter each other there. At least we would have good reason."

Schäkele, a specialist on the matter, takes out a copy of *Le Moniteur des Colonies*, a colonial review based at 8, rue Joubert, Paris. He reads aloud in a sententious tone, with much rolling of his Rs. These are accounts of French explorers. The voyages of the Gentil, the Brazza, the Mizon and the Dybowsky are referred to in the official republican vocabulary as "missions". Inhuman, bloodthirsty, diabolical, cannibalistic, perfidious Negroes rival the beasts in their savagery in lands plagued by mysterious, deadly diseases. I feel as though I am listening to Father talking about the Gauls in Roman times. *Le Moniteur des Colonies* dramatises these massacres. To fearlessly vanquish ... Thereby making the successes all the more heroic. One article talks about the Maison Verdier and its cocoa plantations on the French Côte d'Or, which adjoins the British Gold Coast. Gold! The dreamers fall silent, the sleepers awake.

"At the Manu, they decided to stop trying to convert Chassepots. They're planning to make only new Gras rifles."

The Alsatians take pity on my quizzical countenance.

"The Chassepots are cursed! For all their superiority, they failed to prevent the Prussian debacle. Today, they are outmoded. But there are hundreds of thousands of them still in armouries. We can hardly throw them away ..."

"So, we convert them."

"The chambers of the Chassepots take old-fashioned paper cartridges, which produce too much noise and smoke. In sustained gunfire, a soldier, if he should still be alive, will emerge deaf and blind ..."

"We expand the chamber to allow for more air, reinforce it so that it can withstand metal cartridges and, abracadabra, a Chassepot becomes a Gras."

"Technically, we cannot convert all the Chassepots. It is easier just to make new Gras rifles ..."

"We send the tens of thousands that remain to La Rochelle,

from where they are shipped out to be used in the conquest of the Congo and the Sudan . . ."

"After all, the Negro is less fearsome than the Prussian. Two shots – *bang, bang!* – and he turns tail and flees. We shall have the côte d'or, the côte d'ivoire, the côte de bœuf and any other côte that takes our fancy!"

General laughter.

I ask the assembled company how the rifles are sent to La Rochelle . . .

* * *

"God is a factory boss, the earth is His Manu"; "We say the plight of the workers, we never say the plight of the employers"; "Pray hard to be made a manacle, work hard to become a mechanical"; "The paradise of the manacle is the retirement of the mechanical"; "The church shapes the soul, the factory the body" . . . At the end of the main street, in a tiny insalubrious room, I share a bed with Pierre and his iconoclastic ideas about God, employers and labourers. He often attends the meeting led by Monsieur Krebs, a bayonet fitter who talks of workers' solidarity as of a weapon. "It is as irresistible as a jackhammer. On impact, it creates powerful shockwaves." Pierre takes notes which he later reads to me.

For the first time in my life, I am earning my living. My Alsatian friends make me as efficient as the "no quals". Hefting and cleaning are within everyone's skills. The most difficult thing is getting "called up". Every day, I stand in the same spot outside the workshops, impassive, whatever the weather. The horde of "no quals" pray for one of the erratic appearances of the "bawler", the man who barks out the names and roles of the fortunate few. Religion reigns outside the Manu. "Factories are the new cathedrals. The boss is God, the worker, the creature," dixit Pierre Munchène. I feel ashamed that I am more excited at the thought of stepping inside the Manu then I was when first I set foot inside the cathedral at Tours.

The buildings of the Manu are of gigantic proportions, hollowed Titans lying east–west along the banks of the Vienne. In their bellies, not a wall, not a partition, nothing but serried lines of pillars supporting the sawtooth roofs. The logic guiding the various processes is apparent only to a demi-urge intimately familiar with every trade, workshop, machine, material and product. Work is on an assembly line. Every stage, even the most anodyne, is keenly watched by a super-visor, a sort of sergeant whose role, as in the army, is to bark orders. Above the supervisor are the workshop masters, above whom the controllers of armaments, like Stek, sit enthroned. It is a military hierarchy. They are, after all, manufacturing weapons. Every worker is precisely stationed in the factory and condemned to an endless series of repeated actions, ges-tures and movements. Cleaning, handling, storing, fetching, carrying . . . A "no qual" is not involved in every stage of the production line. He can be summoned to any of the work-shops. I shall describe the places where Pierre has never set foot. Of the forge, of the furnaces, all he knows is what he has heard of the blistering heat and the "cooking" bonus earned by smiths. Of the power hammer, he knows only the noise and the tremors that radiate through the town. Paradoxically, this separation of roles fosters esprit de corps among the workers.

41

The work of one group makes sense only through the work of another. As was clear some nights ago, only when they come together can they precisely describe how a single weapon is made. I understand why word travels so quickly among the groups of workers.

It takes nine months of "bawling" and a dozen "manacles" before I stumble on the opportunity I have been waiting for: a convoy transporting crates of Chassepots and ammunition to La Rochelle. Pitchforked into the role of packer, my job is to strap down or remove the covers from the carts. The Alsatians know that I will not return. In taking my leave from Pierre, I make no solemn promise other than to find his cousin LG. A promise I would have foresworn had I but known that vast scale of Africa, my intended destination ever since my first night in Châteauneuf. But, sometimes, destiny watches over even the most reckless pledges.

* * *

Two days later, La Rochelle. My relief upon our arrival is not simply attributable to the serious discomfort of our means of locomotion. Sitting atop crates of munitions and kegs of gunpowder, I am reminded by every pothole of the propinquity of death in a blaze of fireworks.

The new harbour built in the village of La Pallice is the hub of the town's activity. Straight roads, junctions at right angles – everything has been fashioned to afford easy access to the sea. The teeming dockyards span an area a hundred times greater than the Manu, and the bustle of man and machine is just as frenetic. The carts reach their terminus at the warehouses that overlook the harbour. Carved onto the pediment: "CFK: Compagnie Française de Kong". Pierre's "the Congo". A convergence of signs. A few hours' sweating under the raucous cries of the foreman and our mission is complete. The pile of crates is stacked next to a tree trunk as broad as the height of one man stood upon the shoulders of another. "Alépé 2385" is stencilled on the side. The foreman must surely have shouted himself hoarse the day this piece of lumber was unloaded. An inquisitive workman is censured for his curiosity.

"Don't touch that trunk. You'll infect it with the filth of your shithole. Your great-great-grandfather was not yet born when that tree stood proudly in the forest! In the name of a bedevilled negress, great deaths warrant great respect!"

I approach the howler as he is lambasting the poor wretch.

"Monsieur, if you would be so good, I wish to travel to Africa. Could you direct me to someone who might advise?"

Like a tree falling athwart a river, his flow is instantly staunched. He turns to me, his eyes, his nostrils and his lips fashioning the same round "O". He looks me up and down. Slowly. I cannot look away. I hold his gaze. The feeling of being in a duel: the Chassepots are near at hand. Gradually, the waters rise and dislodge the fallen tree.

"Amédééééééé!"

Never again will my words have such effect.

A pair of elephant tusks frames the window that opens onto the unfinished quadrilateral of the harbour. In the office, the floor is carpeted by a plantation of statues, the walls curtained with masks, the rug is the pelt of some big cat. Amédée

Brétignière, a top-hat-beard-moustache-white-gloves in the manner of Châtellerault's right bank, radiates intelligence, moral strength and gentleness from a face that has an almost feminine beauty. He is pale and speaks slowly, panting after each phrase. Wild beasts, ravenous insects, brutal diseases, suffocating heat, gruelling marches, loneliness . . . His portrait is black indeed. Perhaps he is spurred on by my failure to react. What he is saying kindles no spark in me. The mind reacts only to ideas it can imagine. I'm no more fearful than if I were listening to a tale of ogres. For me, as for Jules Ferry and his Gauche Républicaine senators imbued with a mission to civilise, Africa is unimaginable. It cannot terrify.

Amédée hands me a handwritten form bearing the letterhead of the Compagnie Française de Kong. I append my signature next to that of Arthur Verdier, French resident of Côte de l'Or, Rivières du Sud and its dependencies. Thereafter, Joseph, the bellowing foreman, addresses me at a volume that is bearable, though significantly above that of civilised conversation. Amédée's tales take on a different hue. Proper names begin to appear: "Treich", "Anno", "Anyi", "Krinjabo", "Élima". Amédée is a doctor of law, and I hear much about his legal wrangles with the British. When he broaches the subject of Élima, I allow myself to be guided by the passion in his voice.

"The Élima coffee plantation was one of Arthur's ideas. He sent me to look for coffee plants in Liberia, where his brother Ernest is the French consul. This tiny Black country on the western border of Rivières du Sud was created by the American Colonization Society, a group of philanthropists led by a nephew of George Washington. These white men shipped

Black slaves from America en masse, set them free and, without so much as a by-your-leave, transplanted them to the jungles of Africa, together with plants such as rubber trees, sugar cane and coffee. The Élima school was my idea. One day, an Anyi told me: 'Where plants thrive, the people thrive.' It was this that gave me the vision. At first, Arthur wanted nothing to do with it. But I was sure of getting a subvention from the government. A polite letter to the Ministre de la Marine copied to the lieutenant-governor, and we were assigned a teacher. While we waited for him to arrive, Madame Keller, the wife of our Alsatian foreman, helped me with the initial classes. The schoolmaster, Monsieur Jean-d'heur, arrived shortly before the infection had me sent back here . . ."

Amédée pants for breath. As memories flood back, so too does his illness.

"I cannot stay here. I am eager to return to Treich, to our school, our little white house on the hill above the lake; our giant kapok tree, the three little pigs we named after the three steamships, the *Paul Bert*, the *Chanzy* and the *Jules Ferry*; to our workers who love it when I shout '*Ndè-ndè! Ndè-ndè!*'; all the moments we have shared, Treich and I, far from the prying eyes of the petty colonists in Assinie and Grand-Bassam; our projects, all the prospecting, the topographical surveys to trace a map of the country . . . I have to return to the lives we reinvented far from here. I cannot stay here in La Rochelle. I have nothing to live for here."

A COMMUNARD
CHAPTER

UTA

Water, canals, bridges, houses, cattle, water, canals, bridges, houses, cattle ... outside the train windows of the 9.58 a.m. Amsterdam–Paris, the landscape is flashing past; inside Comrade Papa is speechifying. I know all his speeches by heart, but I listen to just enough to avoid an ideological recovery plan. On the outskirts of Amsterdam, Comrade Papa pulls out the heavy machine gun to mow down the blue-and-white Philips logo on the front of a building. The heavy machine gun involves pumping both fists while his mouth goes "Toof! Toof! Toof!" The light machine gun is both index fingers, one behind the other, with a terse "Tat! Tat! Tat!" The Philips family, part of the Dutch bourgeoisie that collaborated in experiments with fascists during the Little War, which was longer but much more deadly than the Great War. They made their fortune selling light and sound. Disgraceful! Profiting from the fundamental waves of nature! When the proletariat are finally victorious, there'll be executions in the public square. The Philips will be hanged next to their light bulbs over the dance floor of a new dictatorship of the people. Free

49

lighting, free music, free television, free cinema for everyone. Just as the slave labour laws of the Boni-Marrons in the jungle forest were abolished, the sovereign people will abolish the egocentric rights of the haughty and replace them with the rights of the people. "Even the most self-obsessed of art is collective," says Comrade Papa.

In Comrade Papa's catalogue of speeches, the Philips one comes just before the tulips. Tulips are Turkish flowers that caused a fever with the Dutch bourgeoisie a long time ago. Long before the British invented steam, protestanting Dutch burghers used Turkish flowers to make the stalk market. Tulips aren't particularly nice flowers, even sheep won't eat them. But on account of the capital grains, people bought and sold these plants and invented stalk-market capitalism. Capitalism wasn't invented in England, everyone got that wrong, including Marx and his Angles. From the Nether Lands and regions, these weeds spread through country after country, and the stalk market contaminated the whole world. If it hadn't been for Red October, the mighty USSR would have been infected. China was saved by Comrade Mao, who had sturdy calves that could make long marches and great leaps forward to escape epidemics. To Comrade Papa, the Nether Lands is Patient Zero. Like science researchers, he and Maman came here so they could understand Patient Zero and find a vaccine for the world stalk-market disease. It was because of the tulips that I was born in Amsterdam. This is another speech that ends with the public hangings of the capitalist latchkeys and a lot of abolishing.

Water, canals, bridges, houses, cows, water, canals, bridges, houses, cows ... There is no sign of the sovereign people from the windows of the train. Outside, the countryside is still flashing past, inside Comrade Papa is still dashing forward.

In proletarian school, when the teacher asks what's the capital of France, I shout: The Paris Commune! This is a subject that gets Comrade Papa worked up into fits and starts. You can't shut him up. You see, I was born under the sign of Pluto. And that's the worst possible thing because it makes you a plutocrat. According to Comrade Papa, I defied all scientific calculations that I'd get myself born on March 18, the anniversary of the Paris Commune. I was born on January 18.

The Paris Commune started out with songs and flowers and fraternity with the reactionary forces. The people's happiness lasted seventy-two days, and the only thing they missed was fresh bread every morning because the bakers were forced to sleep at night so they could be happy like everyone else. But, just like me being born, the Paris Commune turned out to be premature. A traitor found the parting in some rampart and let thousands of third-rate republicans pour into the city. *A hundred thousand!* shouts Comrade Papa, jabbing ten fingers in the air. All this puts him in a State of Anxiety. He spins out of control when he talks about it.

The Versailles infantrymen are no better than the Zouaves in the hellish colonies of Africa and Asia, whose aim is so perfidious they shoot their own sovereign people. With Thiers as their leader, the rabble from Versailles shoot anything that moves, and hang anyone still standing from the branches of the trees across the City of Light Infantry. The captured Communards are lined up and shot against the walls of the cemetery belonging to Old Father Chaise, so they don't have to worry about transporting the bodies. There aren't many trees up on the Mount of Martyrs, and fewer trees means lots more blood spilled by the sovereign people. So much, in fact, that the Versifailleurs use it to water their vineyards. This is the point when I usually cry a little bit and Comrade Papa is panting so hard his head is nearly touching his belly.

During the three-minute stop at Brussels Gare du Midi, he calmed down and made the most of the opportunity to side-track into the adventures of Leopold Number 2, king of the Belgicans and lord of King Congo. I'm happy, because here in this train carriage is the first time I've spent enough time with Comrade Papa for him to set my ears ringing with the full peal of Philips-Tulips-Paris Commune-Hellish colonies of Africa and Asia. By the time the ticket inspector – a lackey Sick O'Phant of big capitalism – showed up, he'd got to the part in the history of the Congo where there's an international conspiracy against Lumumba the travelling beer salesman. I've always been scared by Africa. It's not only the rivers of blood shed during colonisation, it's Comrade Papa always talking about the horrors of alien nation. I'm starting to think that in Africa there's only lunatics and devils . . .

* * *

"What has to happen always does," says Yolanda. Comrade Papa and I have been together for too long for something strange not to happen. We're right in the middle of my favourite story, about the retching of the earth and the funeral of Doctor Frantz, a Boni-Marron with a black mask and white skin, or vicer verser, who looked after the lunatics in Algeria, when Comrade Papa mutters, "Be quiet." There's a silence like you might hear in the Oude Kerk, filled with the corpses of the lumpenproletariat who had nothing to say when they were alive, let alone now they're dead. It goes on for a really long time, during which our ears are filled with the boogie-woogie clatter of the railway tracks and our eyes with the speeding spectacle of the countryside. He did the same thing the day Maman set off for Comrade Hodja's socialist paradise. And he called me Citizen. Not Comrade, Citizen. That was the first time. This is the second.

"Citizen!"

"Yes, Comrade Papa?"

"Citizen, we are all recruits waiting for the call-up."

"Yes, Comrade Papa, you can call me up. I'm always ready for the revolution!"

"Your maman didn't leave us, she answered the call."

"Yes, Comrade Papa."

"Now that your maman is not here anymore, there's no reason for us to stay."

"Yes, Comrade Papa."

"I know that you are a good little revolutionary and you've got a good head on your shoulders, but I can't leave you to fend for yourself without your mother."

"Yes, Comrade Papa."

"What with the class traitors in social services . . ."

"Yes, Comrade Papa, the class traitors."

"They're capable of sending you off to a foster home, one of the capitalist gulags for children of the proletariat."

"Yes, Comrade Papa."

"I'm working with our French comrades on something very important for the revolution in Africa. We're preparing a coup a little like the *Granma*, the yacht that landed fighters on the coast for the Cuban revolution. It worked for Fidel, it'll work for us."

"Yes, Comrade Papa."

"In the meantime, I need to get you to safety."

"Yes, Comrade Papa."

"Back there in Holland, that's not our home."

". . ."

"Do you understand what I'm saying?"

". . ."

"I need you to understand. We have to prepare our own revolution. We'll do that elsewhere. There's nothing more we can do for the sick capitalist state of the Netherlands."

". . ."

"There, we have no-one, we are no-one."

"Yolanda . . ."

"I can't leave you with her."

"Yolanda?"

"She's not allowed to take care of you. She's not your mother. She's not even family."

"The Boni-Marron tribe is our family."

"Citizen, the Boni-Marron tribe is just a fairy tale. You'll see, there are lots of Yolandas where you're going, they'll take good care of you."

"Lots of Yolandas?"

"Yes. Your uncles, your aunts, your cousins, your grand-mother – your real tribe is there."

"..."

"Citizen, you know I'm proud of you. Your mother is proud of you too. You're the greatest little revolutionary we know."

"..."

"Now listen carefully, I'm sending you on a mission! You're going on a very big adventure. Out in the wide world, you'll be an undercover agent for Maman and me. You're the best, the most beautiful thing we have ever done or read in this life. We're not about to let you fall into enemy hands. Your revolutionary mission is more important than anything."

Startled by my valiant "Yes, Comrade Papa, *vive la révolution!*", the whole carriage turns to see me standing, ramrod straight, fist raised, accepting my mission. I execute a perfect revolutionary salute. Comrade Papa looks at me; in his eyes I see something like pity or embarrassment.

* * *

Barricades: zero, protest marches: zero, partisan songs: zero. No revolutionary zeal, no signs of fraternisation with reactionary forces; Amsterdam Centraal and Gare du Nord are exactly the same. People, not A PEOPLE. Horrible faces. The real Communards must all have been put up against the cemetery wall and shot. All that's left are the third-rate republicans and their leader Thiers, an Adolph like the other one with the swas-stickers. All those bowed heads, but luckily Comrade Papa and the new revolutionaries will chop them off on the day of the big night. The Paris Commune is a disappointment. We head off for the bourgeois airport, with its jet-set planes.

"Air France? Never! They only transport the consumerist

classes. When it comes to the sovereign people, they deport us. Air Afrique? Never! A company of settlers from the hellish alien nation colonies who dream of imitating their masters by serving up French bourgeois jet set with an African sauce. It has to be UTA! Ah, the UTA! The Union of Air Transporters. When you hear the word 'Union', you're never far from the hallowed workers, standing up to evil employers. UTA, the only airline in which all the workers are shareholders. And that's just the beginning. The struggle continues! Soon, the workers will take control. They'll paint the planes in deepest red. Workers at Renault, Matra, Simca and Peugeot will follow their example. Management by the people for the people! In the future, Citizen, every car will be red!"

Comrade Papa is wide awake now after his tacit turn. A new, final speech. We're standing in front of the UTA counter. A lady smiles. She tells me to come with her. She's got dark hair and she doesn't look particularly working-class dressed in her feudal-kings-of-France blue uniform. But I trust Comrade Papa. Especially when he calls me Citizen. He gives me a little wave before I disappear down a long corridor with the lady. Another corridor, a revolving door, a sliding door, a door with a padlock, a security door, through a couple of swing doors and I find myself in an office. I'm given a neck bag in the company feudal-kings-of-France blue. It's got my name written in black marker. The letters are round and curvy like Maman's handwriting, only not as pretty. The woman from the counter is nice and asks me what I want to drink.

"Coke, Pepsi, Fanta, 7-Up, Miranda, Dr Pepper, Squirt, Orangina?"

I'm really thirsty, but I reject these capitalist consumer drinks. I say nothing. Another lady in feudal-kings-of-France blue comes over. This one looks like a third-rate republican management latchkey. A monster. She bends down, peers at me, asks a few questions that I don't answer. In the end, she bursts out laughing and says I've got the face of a retard, like all Black kids. Except that I'm not a kid, or a retard, or Black. Her blond hair is just within reach. Result: hair-pulling and class warfare. Moody Marko would have appreciated it. The monster howls. I burst into tears. I'm crying about everything: Maman, Comrade Papa, Yolanda, the window women, Marie-Anna's gang, De Wallen, the proletarian primary school, the class wars, the teachers, the red lights, the revolution . . . I'm bawling about everything. Even Moody Marko. I don't know how long this went on, but for ages afterwards, I still had a fistful of blond hair. The dark-haired lady from the counter and the corridors and doors and stuff does her best to comfort me. She never gets too close, but she never leaves my side, she even goes with me onto the plane. I'm not impressed, I'm still blubbing. She belts me into a seat. She's probably afraid I'll do a runner like Yolanda's Boni-Marrons in the jungle. When she shows me a sick bag, I suddenly stop crying. The lady from the check-in counter and the corridors and doors, etc., looks surprised. She wipes my face and makes me blow snotty air into a handkerchief of slave-picked cotton. She's very busy bustling about me. I'm starting to see the working class in her. I ask her for my school satchel, and take out one of the sweets Yolanda gives to children. The rest I put in the sick bag and set it down next to me. I kiss the sweet, then take out

Maman's book. The cover is red. The title is in silver letters: *Literature and the Revolutionary Arts*. The name of the writer is in gold: Kim Il Sung. On the second to last page, opposite Maman's seven tenets, in my neatest literature handwriting, I write: *Mama is in de socialistische hemel, Kameraad papa is naar de Parijse Commune, En ik vertrek naar de hel van de Afrikaanse en Aziatische kolonies.* "Maman is in socialist heaven, Comrade Papa is in the Paris Commune. And I'm leaving for the hell of the African and Asian colonies."

The Legend of the
Prince and Parisian

There was a man from the Auvergne named Gonzalves who was eager to advance his fortunes and to curry favour with King Louis XIV. In Assinie, known at that time as Issiny, the capture of young Negro boys sparks an idea. Aniaba is a handsome and quick-witted lad. Gonzalves presents him to the royal court as prince of an African kingdom as vast, as wealthy and as sophisticated as Egypt. Aniaba is tutored at the palace of Versailles, receives his First Communion from the Archbishop of Paris and becomes Hannibal, Prince of Issiny. "There is no more difference twixt you and me than twixt black and white!" quips Louis XIV one morning while hunting to hounds. Everyone believes him to be a prince. The young man ends up believing it himself. By the time he returns to his native lands, he is the captain of a cavalry regiment in Hainaut. With great pomp and fanfare, a battleship and two frigates tasked with transporting him home to his kingdom set sail from La Rochelle. The armada drops anchor off the coast of Assinie in June, the worst season for crossing the bar.

The apostolic prefect for the coast of Guinea, the captain, the ship's lieutenant . . . the grand cortège representing the kingdom of France board a small skiff and go to proclaim the prince's homecoming. They are cast into the depths by the first breakers. Recognised by his agemates, Aniaba becomes kangah, house slave to the king of Krinjabo. Then and there, amid riotous laughter, he is stripped of his garments, his honours and medals, his weapons and regalia. Only his shoes find no takers. He is thrown to the crabs in the mangrove swamps and given a pagne to cover his private parts, which, in the manner of Versailles, are shamefully shaven. As for France, it has naught but a sandbar caught between ocean and lagoon. The delegates, having publicly escaped death with nothing to show but their sodden finery, are suddenly less brash in negotiations. Using planks from the two frigates, they build a fort. The captain leaves, promising to return with fresh supplies. There is no more talk of Aniaba.

In the sand, nothing grows. It is a group of naked white men who, four years later, are hailed by the captain of a passing ship from Normandy. He is determined to take his compatriots home, with no negotiations and no payment of tribute. The affronted Assinians overrun the beach, sit down, as in a theatre, and wait. Miraculously, the skiff manages to make the crossing. Of the hundred men who came as escort to Aniaba, there are only eight survivors. One of their number, Parisian, much favoured by the natives, decides to remain. The other seven set off back to the sandbar and, after four years of waiting, hoping, fuming and suffering, are drowned, as the dumbfounded Norman captain looks on.

Since that time, from Assinie as far as the Cape of the Jack-

Jack by way of Grand-Bassam, when a white man proves himself valiant and curious about the country, he is called "Parisian". When he is untrustworthy, people say that he is "French".

AN UNCLE TOM CHAPTER

on the COLONIAL TEMPERAMENT

The crossing is a memory of dizziness, nausea, gastric and hepatic catastrophes in every combination of "and/or". I do not set foot outside the cabin I share with a few shipping trunks, a family of rats, a tribe of cockroaches and fetid smells from the hold mingled with those from the smokestack. Since leaving port, my movements have been limited to trudging back and forth between my berth and the toilet bucket into which I vomit bile and viscera. Whereas the average man over-comes seasickness within a few hours of turmoil, here I am, days later, still spewing up my guts. Continuously. A number of the crew have been considerate enough to provide me with some care, which amounts to wiping my face with a damp flannel. The toilet bucket is rarely emptied. The foul stench is compounded by my own miasma.

Shaken by the pitching and rolling, dazed from the constant lurching, exenterated by the vomiting, and light-headed from the tossing, I believe I overhear someone complain that I am dying, since my demise will precipitate an obligatory stop at the nearest French outpost, where the British crew will have to report my death to the authorities. Those are the rules. The captains in His Majesty's merchant marine prefer to avoid French trading posts and their protracted bureaucratic formalities and have consequently adopted the custom of salting the bodies of French citizens who die under their ensign. The corpses are thus preserved until they reach the next British trading post where a simple declaration is sufficient to rid themselves of the remains. I have no desire to end up like a codfish. I plan to hold out until I hear the call of "Grand-Bassam!"

The cabin is cluttered with twenty or so packages destined for divers trading houses, the jute sack from the Post Office, the briefcase I hurriedly purchased at a market in La Pallice, two trunks emblazoned with MAC followed by four numbers, and me, the lone human being, if I can still be referred to as such. I have to be carried ashore. Up on deck, I think I see relief in the faces of the crew. I summon my last vestige of dignity and a little strength to refuse the barrel used to put ashore the cripples, the maimed and the dying. I cling to the sides of the basket lowering me into the pirogue.

From frying pan to flame: the little boat pitches and rolls more brutally than the cargo ship. The guts that survived the ship begin to churn more wildly. I curl into a ball, staring vacantly, my vision fragmented. Bare feet, Black backs, a puddle in the dugout, a bailer, a glimpse of oars, flecks of sea foam . . . With each lurch, I am more convinced that my last moments are at hand. I pray. This will be my final paternoster. As if I were at Mass, as I utter the final words, I hear voices singing. Here, in the maelstrom of Poseidon, the eddies of

Neptune, the slime of the Puits-du-diable, men are singing. Truly, God speaks Latin, He has heard my prayer. Overcome, I muster a little courage, I raise my head. Above the dancing prow, I see alternating lines and curves. The song grows louder, the land draws nearer. The earth, harsh mother, constant mother, does not move, does not sway, does not try to disembowel her children. Land ho! Everything sings. I struggle to my feet and dive into the waves that have had my guts heaving for sixteen days now. I do not swim. I flail at the sea, lashing out with hands and feet, pounding the waves. Revenge. My eyes have returned to their sockets. There are people next to me. Seven or eight – I find I can count once more. The oarsmen have dived in too. This is no tragedy, but rather a celebration. We are lifted by a wave; the shore is fast approaching. I am not dead, I am laughing. Loudly. My beached neighbours gather around and laugh with me. Loudly. One of them comes closer. With one hand he claps my back and with the other beats the most muscular chest I have ever seen.

"Me Wayou."

"I am Dabilly."

"Dabii?"

"Dabilly."

His palm still raining blows upon my spine, he calls out to his comrades: "Dabii! Dabii!" I fall into their arms, one by one. The man slapping my back assumes the attitude of a medieval lord who has won a joust.

"Me James Clarck Vandernels Fredericssen de Oliveira Wayou. You good man, Dabii."

* * *

A single glance is enough to take in the whole of Grand-Bassam. The designation is incongruous. The shore is a narrow sandbank beaten by waves that runs parallel to the larger street, a simple line of trading houses and commercial buildings. Some twenty metres further on, a smaller street is lined with palm-thatched houses. The remaining thoroughfares are a tangle of dirt tracks rutted through the stunted vegetation. A lagoon, scarcely wider than the River Creuse, marks the northern boundary of the town.

The landing stage for the pirogues is called the port. The first trading house on the main street is a stone building housing the CFAO, the Compagnie Française de l'Afrique de l'Ouest, a specialist in all manner of trafficking, only recently incorporated. Next to this is the impressive wrought-iron building of the West Afrikans Telegraph Company Limited (the herculean British plan to link all West African trading posts by telegraphy, and Grand-Bassam is to be a major hub), the trading house of Swanzy & Co., and the warehouses of Woodin & Co., the British textile specialists. Surrounded by a single palisade, these four comprise the British Compound. Next to this, a string of small Marseillaise stores, heirs to the old company of Régis Aîné, offer no sign as to their commercial purpose. Further along are the well-known trading houses SCOA (Société Commerciale de l'Ouest Africain), King & Co., and CCCA (Compagnie Commerciale des Côtes d'Afrique). British trading houses have proper names, while the French favour acronyms. At the far end of the street, the CFK (Compagnie Française de Kong) is a hulking building flanked by two stone pavilions like defensive bastions.

68

The founder, Arthur Verdier, purchased what was the Fort Nemours for a pittance when Napoleon III ordered his cannon fodder to return home to be slaughtered on the banks of the Meuse. It is now called Fort Verdier. I am billeted in a room in the north pavilion.

My neighbour, a man by the name of Bricard, is administrative officer, chief customs officer, tax collector and postmaster, together with many other roles that are awaiting civil servants to be dispatched from France. "We have a duty to accelerate the arrival of settlers"; "We have a duty to stave off the British peril"; "We have a duty to save our coastal trading posts"; "We have a duty to preserve the fruits of our labours" ... Bricard's frequent use of the word "duty" neatly chimes with his character and with the popular image of the personal secretary to the duly appointed French resident minister. Bricard is the right-hand man of the most important person in the colony. But whether "we" refers to the French Republic or simply to the Verdier trading house is unclear. He informs me that I will be assigned "a post in a forested area north of Assinie". In this uncharted territory, I am to build and run a trading post. I know nothing of bureaucratic paperwork, have only a superficial understanding of trade, have never worked as a civil servant, am utterly ignorant of the regulations governing construction, and my military knowledge begins and ends with protecting my henhouse from foxes; but none of these failings is a cause for concern.

"Everything here needs to be invented, beginning with ourselves." What of the precise location where I am to set up this post? "Treich is the only man who has ventured so far. He will guide you." What of the date of my mission? "Treich will decide. He is always in favour of allowing time for people to acclimatise." All questions lead to Treich, the French resident minister. The man is a saint. Treich knows. Treich understands. Treich decides. Treich dares. Treich moves. Those here do not talk about him, they *invoke* him. His name, pronounced with a final whisper, adds to his mystique: Treicccchhhh!

* * *

The erstwhile Issiny of Aniaba, self-styled African prince, genuine French prince, is now Assinie, the seat of the Résidence de France, a day's walk to the east of Grand-Bassam. While waiting to meet with Treich there, I acclimatise. I make contact with a man named Dejean, a Verdier agent who, like all the others, has multiple roles. He is responsible for the induction and training of new arrivals, for recruiting native porters and for bringing together the equipment necessary for exploratory missions. I find him in the main warehouse talking to a Black man, short in stature, dressed in the Western style, whom he introduces as his interpreter. Dejean calls him Saint-Pierre. Barely have I started to wonder why an interpreter is required for a conversation between two men who speak the same language before Dejean launches into a long litany, which is illuminated by the antics of Saint-Pierre. Mocking, outraged, serious, dramatic, supportive ... the interpreter's facial expressions capture Dejean's every mood.

"Uniforms, white linen: six; uniforms, khaki: six. Flannel suits for the cooler season: four. Oh yes, monsieur, we have a cold season and you can catch a cold. When you are accustomed to months at thirty degrees, 25°C in the shade feels like freezing. Besides, our enemy is not the thermometer, it's the hygrometer. At very high humidity, the air carries telluric miasmas, which are the poisons of these places. Right, to continue . . ."

Commercial buildings and trading houses are built to a specific standard. Shops and offices on the ground floor. Living room, dining room and bedrooms with balconies on the first floor. An adjoining building serves as a warehouse or workshop. A compound of lath-and-plaster huts housing the Black "boys", who tend to the farmyard and the vegetable garden. There may also be huts and tents reserved for itinerant labourers, porters, pedlars, etc. The whole complex to be surrounded by a fence of woven palm branches or a white-washed bamboo palisade.

"Helmets: two. Chosen for their insulation and lightness – cork is the best material we've found. Make sure your helmet covers the back of your neck. Never go out without a helmet before 6 p.m., even if the sky is overcast. The tropical sun is dangerous, particularly when you cannot see it. Right, let's move on . . ."

Between the trading houses, side streets are clustered with the dwellings of the Black population. The most numerous are the Apollonians who hail from the neighbouring British Gold Coast. Though they are statuesque, the name does not come from the Greek god. Legend has it that a Portuguese sailor first encountered them on the day of Santa Apolonia, the virgin martyr Saint Apollonia. Wherever white people settle, they are ever-present, selling their labour or exercising

71

their commercial acumen. Almost all the goods we sell pass through Apollonian hands before reaching our territory. Their partners are the Mandé-Dyula pedlars, which term covers a constellation of ethnic groups ranging from the Malinké in the depths of Guinea to the Soninke on the borders of the Sahara. They cover extraordinary distances on foot, carrying bales of goods perched atop their heads – European goods into the hinterland, and African goods towards the coast. In our trading with the Guineas, the Apollonians are our hands, the Mandé-Dyula our feet.

"Walking boots: two pairs. Casual shoes, or city shoes: one pair. Without shoes, you're fair game for chiggers. They burrow beneath your toenails and suck your blood until they are the size of peas. Walking boots should rise to sixteen centimetres above the ankle. Most snake bites occur below that point. Right, let's move on . . ."

The shoreline is a succession of shelters for the pirogues and their crews. Each trading house has its own flotilla. But the boats have increased in number and one in two runs aground on the sandbar. A nightmare for the trading houses. They have no choice but to employ Krumen, the surest and most efficient crews. Solid as rocks, supple as reeds, they are kings of the coast. They hail from a coastline between Cape Palmas and the San Andrea river, a hundred thousand nautical miles to the west of Grand-Bassam. The Kru have been sailing with Europeans for centuries, since the time of the first Dutch, Danish, Portuguese and British ships. They have never displayed the fear or apprehension of other Black peoples in their encounters with the White man. Hence their reputation for insolence. For this reason, the Portuguese dubbed their country the Costa do Mala Gens, the coast of the evil men. It was the British who bestowed the tribal name: "Crewmen". Traditionally, the Krumen adopt the first names of all the captains with whom they have worked. The most experienced hands have lengthy names drawn from all over Europe, like my new friend James Clarck Vandernels Fredericssen de Oliveira Wayou.

An Apollonian pirogue consists of a helmsman and six oarsmen, while the Krumen use an extra oarsman on the starboard side. Apollonians brave the waves, attacking them head-on; Krumen yield to the wave, approaching it aslant. The Apollonian trajectory is straight, perpendicular to the beach; that of the Krumen is curved, tending westward. When a wave hits, the Apollonian boat rears up while the Krumen arches its back. Apollonian oarsmen despise the stolid Krumen. The Krumen have nothing but contempt for the hard-working Apollonians.

"Toiletries: a complete range. Impeccable personal hygiene is a requisite. Two baths per day, preferably during daylight. My predecessor, Chirac, dared to bathe one night in the path of driver ants – voracious insects that can dispatch a giant boa in a scant few hours, so they made short work of a man from Corrèze. Right, let's move on . . ."

As in all French towns, a cemetery extends from the outskirts of Grand-Bassam. Two lines of coconut palms pay tribute to the dead. Crosses rise above the mounds of red earth covered in brown seaweed. The names carved on crossbars with knives are mostly French. A dozen, perhaps, are English.

One is inset with a miraculous medal of the Black Madonna: "Roman Wieschiewski – 1863". Probably a Pole. Only the year of death appears on the graves. The years 1870 and 1871 were particularly prolific. A spate of epidemics. Yellow fever. There are no indigenous names. I do not know where the natives bury their dead.

"Folding camp bed with mosquito net. The mosquito is our foremost enemy, deadlier than the Negro and the wild beast. Swarms of airborne executioners. Each bite can lead to bilious haemoglobinuric fever, the last stage of malarial cachexia. Everything is spotted with blood: vomit, faeces, urine. You end up a skeleton in boots. Doctor Péan himself could not assuage it. This doctor of dysentery-ridden arseholes has but one piece of advice: four-quarters! A quarter grain of quinine at four o'clock each day. Heed his advice. Without quinine, you have no chance of passing the 'two/two' mark: only two white men in ten survive two years. As to the other eight, this devourer of Black arses is a past master in penning eulogies. Right, let's move on ..."

With the sea to the south, the mouth of the Comoé to the east and the lagoon to the north, Grand-Bassam is accessible by land only from the trading post of Azuretti to the west. Bricard looks at me quizzically when I ask if it is an Italian trading post. I want to go there. He makes some muttered comment about my youth. Azuretti will be my first escapade as an explorer. Though it is a mere half-hour's walk along the shore, I set off feeling as though I have something of Henry Morton Stanley beneath my helmet and in my shorts. "Azuretti?" I say to anyone I encounter, which is pretty much the whole village, eager to ensure that I have reached my destination. "Nzué Ti! Nzué Ti!" echoes a native, gesticulating broadly. He points to a water basin. A neophyte explorer, I did not even think to bring a flask. A poor Stanley indeed! I nod in agreement, and the man flings his arms wide in despair. He points at the water, shouting, "Nzué," then at his head, "Ti," before plunging it into the basin. I get the picture. The Azuretti on our maps is Nzué-Ti, "head in the water". Stanley, taste not of this Pierian Spring.

"Filters: half a dozen cartridges. Water is life. There is an abundance of life in these parts. It invites itself into the smallest drop of water, ready to blossom in the intestines. Diarrhoea is a godsend. The alternative is dysentery, otherwise known as "shitting your guts out"! Always wash your hands before you eat. Always use cutlery. Right, let's move on . . ."

At Nzué-Ti, I spend a whole day engaged in mime. The hilarity prompted by my every gesture tells me much about myself. Gesture and laughter are a universal language. By the time I make my way home, the dusk is gathering. The red disc of the sun hangs suspended for a moment above the horizon, then suddenly plunges into the sea. All around, with no gradation, night falls. Literally. On the outskirts of Grand-Bassam, there are lighted oil lamps in the barracks, in the Black compound. From every side, I am met with greetings, invectives, invitations. The more daring block my path, merely to exchange a handshake. "M'sieur Dabii, Chef Dabii, Patron Dabii . . ." In only a few short days, it seems that everyone recognises me, even in the dark of this moonless night. A shadow stops me. The imposing build is not hard to identify. Wayou and his friendly claps on the back. I cough in anticipation.

"Smoked kidneys: no need. Though the sun bathes this accursed country, only the trees reap the benefit, and you will be beneath them. They can be used in the savannahs of the Great North, but first you must cross this forest from one side to the other. I shall wear a pair, you never know. Now, let's move on ..."

In La Rochelle, I saw a Black man. Dressed as he was like a fine gentleman, it was some time before I noticed his colour. Here in Grand-Bassam, barely clothed Black bodies are ever on display. Squat or lanky, fat or thin, the anatomies vary, but all are distinguished by bulging muscles, even some of the women. In this dusky throng, the White Man looks pale and sickly. From the moment you land on the beach, the exposed flesh attracts the eyes and indeed other organs. Europeans are embarrassed by the near-nakedness of Black women. Most wear only a pagne. When tied beneath their breasts, it barely covers the upper thighs; tied at the waist, the breasts are left exposed. Whether flowing and multicoloured after the British fashion, or stiff and monochrome as tradition dictates, in the pagne the African woman finds poses that would be the envy of our most intoxicating bourgeois ladies.

Young girls and less well-to-do women wear only a simple square of cloth as a cache-sexe. In Grand-Bassam, the height of coquetry is a kerchief bearing the image of Queen Victoria slipped between the thighs. The elderly monarch's face sways in a place that British propaganda could never have imagined. Black women are unembarrassed by the eyes of men. To the naive mind, their innocent manner might suggest a clear invitation. I use all the arsenal of my imagination so as not to see them. My greatest fear is that my confusion will make itself public. How do others get by?

"Long walks and intense physical activities can produce mental deficiencies. The colonialist should not imperil himself by too much thinking. Long periods spent reading are not recommended. If he should miraculously survive the external threats, his greatest enemy is within . . ."

Saint-Pierre, mouth gaping, slowly moves his head up and down. Dejean, with a conspiratorial air, waits for his interpreter to complete his mime with a roll of his eyes and a whisper.

"Colonial cockroaches make men eccentric, tetchy, presumptuous, maudlin, rowdy, irascible, unsociable, misanthropic, cantankerous, garrulous, prolix, disquisitious . . ."

For each adjective, Saint-Pierre finds a facial expression.

"Just look at Doctor Péan . . ."

The face of an inquisitor content at having delivered a sentence without right of appeal.

"Now go away, future dysenteric! I will prepare everything. There are white men here today, and, through my good graces, there always will be. Before long, I shall be governor, my good man, governor."

He stands up, turns his back, his arms folded, his blond hair falling over the back of his sunburnt neck.

"Mandé-Dyulas, come here!"

"Mandé-Dyulaaaaaaaas, come heeeeeeeeere!"

I take my leave of the two men, without really having understood their little game.

* * *

In Fort Verdier, my roommate Bricard is so discreet anyone might think he did not live there. The polar opposite of Dejean, who can be heard screaming in the south wing at all hours of the day and night. Some man named Dreyfus – no-one is sure whether he is a scientist or a prospector – occupies the room usually reserved for Sire Verdier himself. As he has aged, the French resident minister no longer travels below a latitude of 43°N – that is to say, on a par with Marseille. As a young man, he spent ten years living on the Guinea coast, five years straight between Grand-Bassam and Assinie. No European has survived such a prolonged sojourn with his mental faculties intact. But Verdier is still sharp-witted and thriving, still trafficking with African affairs in the salons and halls of La Rochelle, Paris, London and Amsterdam. In Grand-Bassam, he is an icon even more revered than Treich. His room is cleaned and made up every day. To be caught unprepared by his sudden arrival – however unexpected – would be sacrilege. It is allocated to others only on presentation of a letter personally signed by him. Accordingly, Dreyfus enjoys an exceptional status. He moved in and installed a collection of rock fragments, an assortment of glass jars, a battery of chemical reagents stored in phials, a panoply of instruments he alone knows how to use. I cannot help but wonder by what miracle all these things crossed the sandbar. Wayou knows how to keep important boats from capsizing.

Opposite Dejean's quarters, Doctor Péan is the sole occupant of a small house that he has elevated to the status of "HOSPITAL", inscribed in blue on a whitewashed sign. "It is the doctor that makes the hospital," he explains, "not the other way round." His surgery is very busy, and the natives are fascinated by the White Man's medicine. Among the many documented diseases are fictitious ailments invented to get the doctor's attention. You should see the smiles on their face as they emerge from their "consultations", flaunting blue iodine patches or immaculately bandaged limbs. There is always a huge crowd outside Péan's surgery, which is to say outside Dejean's quarters. The sick, the hypochondriacs, the maimed and the onlookers, all of whom drive Dejean to distraction. Whenever he heads off to his stores, no-one is allowed to brush past him. "Vomitooooo! Vomitooooo! Vomitooooo!" he bellows, terrified of contagion. The Spanish refer to yellow fever as *vomito negro*. Saint-Pierre clears a path, elbowing his way through the crowd, echoing: "Vomitooooo! Vomitooooo! Vomitooooo!" This twice-daily ballet is well established. Dejean should also schedule a visit to Doctor Péan for at least one or two consultations concerning his mental health. But the two men are so ill-disposed they scarcely take the time to greet each other.

Fourcade, the company accountant, lives and works on the ground floor of the main building. They say he shares a bedroom with the company safe. Two militiamen stand guard outside his quarters. Senegalese men so tall that the Chassepots at their feet look like duelling pistols. Fourcade takes delivery of merchandise from deep inland which he exchanges for goods from France. Each transaction entails theatrical negotiations, not only on the price but on the method of payment. For the Negroes, gold dust has only a social value and is sold only under special conditions. The cowrie, a shell from the Indian Ocean, is sometimes used as currency, but it requires whole basketfuls to purchase a small mirror. The *manillas* worn by forest men, a bronze armlet weighing some hundred and fifty grams, is worth barely twenty French centimes. Using them to trade in palm oil or ivory is nightmarish. More often, it requires more porters to carry the *manillas* than it does the merchandise. *Billons* have proved a great success, but have only recently been introduced. While the colony waits for a real currency, almost all transactions involve cases of gin, bales of tobacco, bolts of cotton, cartons of eau de cologne, barrels of gunpowder, rifles . . . The good old barter system. Fortune favours the shrewd. Fourcade invites me along to the trading floor. It's a great opportunity to find out more about the real reason for our presence here.

"In a single day's walk, you encounter various ethnic groups who understand each other about as well as a churchyard pigeon understands a priest. I need Claude, Zéphirin and Ludovic, but I'm appalled by the barbaric pidgin they pass off as French. It does me good to listen to you."

The colony makes people demanding.

"Their names are unpronounceable and they positively adore ours. So there is no let-up. Not a day goes by without someone begging to be given a Christian name. I baptise them as a reward for their efforts. They vie with each other to become Alfred, Benoît or Prosper."

The colony makes people Baptists.

"We all have two sets of weighing scales, one for buying, one for selling. The first is set to weigh lighter, the second

80

heavier. These people are clever, but they haven't worked that out yet."

In the colony, people profiteer.

"Don't assume that they are naive. These monkeys never pass up an opportunity to cheat us. We've bought countless bales of rubber, cotton and palm kernels weighed down with stones."

The colony makes people just.

"We are all here to fill the coffer and line our pockets in the process. I'm the cashier. I'm not just the treasurer, I personally count the money. No-one spends more time counting than I do. Before long, I'll be governor, lad, governor . . ."

* * *

At dinner, all the Verdier employees gather in the dining hall of the main building. A varied menu, heavy on sauces, light on carefully chosen guests. Braised mutton or goatmeat, poule-au-pot, game stew. All hunting is done by several infantrymen and a few settlers. The surrounding forest is a veritable vivarium. Even the most inept marksman could not come home empty-handed. Pheasant, wild duck, pigeon, deer, antelope, wild boar, hare . . . Our traditional French game is found here in shapes and sizes that suggest they are of a different species. The disparities between animals are like those between people. The ducks here are puny but the pigeons look like birds of prey; the deer are stunted while the hares look like sheep; our wild boars are monsters compared to the piglet-sized cousins we find here . . . We also slaughter creatures that no-one in a French household would even dream of cooking: porcupines, hedgehogs, pythons, crocodiles, monitor lizards, armadillos, giant anteaters, vipers, hippos, monkeys, pangolins, chimpanzees . . . The sea, the lagoons and the rivers teem with fish. Yams and plantains are easy substitutes for potatoes. Cabbage, carrots, green beans, radishes and other European vegetables are sometimes served with dinner. The "boys" are not simply cooks, they are also skilled in growing the seeds we give them. At Fort Verdier, every meal is a banquet at Château Conty, minus the vintage wines.

The chef is called Eugène Cébon. It was Verdier himself who devised the name. Being showered with compliments at every meal, "Eugène, c'est bon!" became Eugène Cébon. As the chief companion to the great man from La Rochelle, Eugène is feared by the other boys. When he barks an order in his broken French, the others stand to attention and shout: "Oui, sèf!" Only one person refuses to participate in this bellicose game. The lone woman in the kitchen maintains a leisurely gait that makes her slender body sway through the corridors of the mess hall. Her almond eyes are riveted to the ground, four tousled braids tumble from her head, her breasts are on display, her belly is scarified with stars, her skin is a deep black.

Eugène invariably wears a Phrygian cap, and his oversized sailor's jersey is tied at the waist with a British kerchief, from which emerge the bowed legs of a former horseman who wears no boots, indeed no shoes at all. At every meal, he stands unblinkingly in front of the table until a guest says: "Eugène, c'est bon!" Since entering Verdier's service, he has only deigned to accept compliments from the highest-ranking guest according to a scale that only he understands. To the general fury of others, only Doctor Péan can move him. When the doctor is absent, he turns to Dejean, much to the resentment of Fourcade. And so it goes.

The seating plan is set in stone. Bricard and Péan sit on one side, Dejean and Fourcade on the other, Dreyfus and I sit at either end. Fourcade explains to me that the former are Negrophiles, the worst kind of white men from the colonies. Péan explains that his opposite neighbours are Negrophobes, the worst kind of white men from the colonies. Negrophobes use "Negroes" for the native men, "Negresses" for the women and "savages" for groups. They pronounce "Negro" with chin raised in an air of superiority, turning up the corners of their lips as they emphasise the "e". The final "s" of "Negress" is drawn out in a libidinous grin. The word "savage" is uttered with wide eyes and a wrinkled nose to conjure up the image. Negrophiles, on the other hand, employ a panoply of epithet-rich noun phrases. "Senegalese infantrymen", "Mandé-Dyula porters", "strapping Krumen", "pretty Apollonian girls", "beautiful Fanti", "wily Malinké", "stunning mulatto women", "horrible Akapless". They know each tribe, each people and do not hesitate to make sweeping generalisations. When I'm asked for my opinion, I muddle up the references. *In medio stat virtus.*

To the Negrophobes, "The Negro is ignorant, the only thing he understands is a kick up the arse." To the Negrophiles, "The Negro is a big child, he needs to be educated with the firm but fair authority of a father." The tropics favour cut-and-dried philosophies. Nuance is never appropriate. When the subject of women rears its head, these camps dissolve and new lines are drawn based on old grudges. Dejean and Péan regularly come close to fisticuffs. The tension is relieved only when the British are mentioned. A shared loathing of the British moderates the tone.

"Those perfidious, thieving, renegade bastards! Four military blockades in the space of a decade. Impossible to load or unload so much as a needle. We lost 1,623,444 francs!"

"Do you know what those degenerates tried to do?"

"You tell me."

"Those whoresons of the queen wanted us to trade Grand-Bassam, Assinie, Lahou, the whole of the Côte d'Ivoire for the Gambia. With Senegal, that would have given us a single bloc, but they would have had the whole Gulf of Guinea."

"Is there gold in Gambia?"

"Can you imagine the British trading gold mines? It's as barren as a rock and peopled by ugly, polygamous Mohammedan Negroes. Simply sustaining the colony costs them almost two million a year. A money pit! They wanted rid of it. No-one fools a Fourcade with phoney figures."

"Fortunately, old man Verdier stuck to his guns. Ten years duping the British is a real feat."

"And dear old Amédée Brétignière? They say that in less than six months, he has produced a report on our border disputes with the Gold Coast of such brilliance that even Her Gracious Majesty has pricked up her ears."

"You should have seen the disappointment on the faces of the British commissioners. Amédée's document detailed everything down to the last banana plant."

"And still the British continue to taunt us. Honestly, selling those horrible fabrics to our Blacks."

"I don't understand what our Negroes see in their gaudy coloured fabric. Now they've started selling them eau-de-cologne. Cologne . . . in the name of every rutting Apollonian! After everything the barbaric Prussians did to us. Now that is what I call a provocation."

"The real threat from the British is the alcohol. Only a Negro could prefer gin to wine. They're going to turn into raving alcoholics."

"They have Apollonian spies wreaking havoc in the royal courts."

"Old Johnson, the fat pervert at Woodin & Co., dared to tell me that if we should have an uprising, they won't just sell gunpowder to the Negroes. They will hand out guns as revenge for what we did to the Ashanti. The nerve! If we only had an administrative council, I'd have him forcibly expelled."

"The administrative council will be restored, my friends. I saw some paperwork in Dakar. There is some great explorer coming from the north. A military man, a former aide-de-camp to Marshal Faidherbe himself. His name is Binger."

"Everyone knows that. We've been hearing about him for the past year. If the Negroes haven't eaten him, he must have died from one of the local diseases. In fact, I heard he had been posthumously decorated. Unless we do something, the British have a bright future ahead."

Only in times of great crisis or in war can such trenchant expressions of nationalism be heard in the metropole. Overweening patriotism is the chief characteristic of the colonist.

To cries of "God save the Mushroom Queen", Negrophobes and Negrophiles alike laugh at the fashion for slipping Victoria between the thighs of the women of Grand-Bassam.

* * *

Hewn from solid wood, with quicklime painted on its legs to ward off termites, and mosquito netting hung from the four corners of the frame, my bed is a fortress. Beneath the pristine sheets I can hear swarms of mosquitoes attack the netting. From time to time, a high whine reminds me that some penetrate this defence system. These fortunate flies will gorge themselves on blood, but will not live to enjoy it. Their abdomens swollen with the proceeds of their crime, they will end up as red stains on the sheets, crushed by my restless sleep in the oppressive heat.

The sound of the surf is not always a lullaby. At times, the sandbar thunders with crashing waves as loud as the hammer blows at the Manu. What the jackhammer is to Châtellerault, the sea is to Grand-Bassam. The whole shoreline quakes when the mother wave hits. But for several consecutive nights, the usual sounds are joined by a commotion that is more domestic than industrial. The first time, it comes from Bricard's house. Sounds of a struggle, a woman screaming, a tirade of insults, the sound of running feet.

"The vicious bitch! She bit me!"

Another night, downstairs, in Fourcade's strongroom.

"That bloody bitch!"

A few nights later, Dejean's instantly recognisable voice:

"The bitch! I'll kill her!"

I wake with a start to the sound of a shotgun blast. But gales of laughter from the boys' compound indicates that the scene is more burlesque than tragic. The following day, after lunch, determined to satisfy my curiosity, I venture into Eugène Cébon's territory. My sudden appearance surprises both my hosts and myself. Three small steps from my bedroom, a world uncharted by any white man. If someone needs something, they have only to shout; it is the colonial's principal mode of communication. The order echoes down the halls of hierarchy to the person responsible and the desire, however trivial, is gratified. When I step into the compound, it is crowded. Everything is instantly suspended, each movement, each gesture. Eugène is the least surprised. He offers me a seat. I refuse with a thank you.

"No thank-you. Sit!"

His tone is firm but benign. I take one of the stools at which he jabs a finger. Hardly have I started to explain the purpose of my visit when he interrupts, bringing the same finger to his lips.

"Shh!"

Stern but benign. He hands me half a hollow, dry gourd. The murky liquid inside looks like water. Use of European utensils, prohibition of unfiltered water, Dejean's preaching guides my second refusal.

"No, thank you."

"No thank-you. Drink!"

Stern but benign. I bring the gourd to my lips. A fresh drink with a lemony aftertaste, a powerful thirst-quencher in this heat. I drain the vessel.

"You drink again."

A few laughs relax the surrounding faces. Eugène pours again. When I have drained it, I do as I have seen the Krumen do on the beach, I turn the gourd upside down and hand it back. According to Wayou-the-back-slapper, this is the most polite way of saying that you have drunk your fill. Distractedly, I mutter a few Latin phrases while I watch the liquid drain into the sandy soil. The laughter dies away. The circle closes around me, everyone shifts closer. Eugène's eyes look sterner still. I fear I have unwittingly flouted some injunction. I am ready to apologise. I know all about contrition. Eugène pounces on my outstretched hand and roughly shakes it.

"Krumen Wayou him say me himself."

My hand is crushed. Long suspended seconds like a threat.

"You good man. Krumen Wayou speak true. You come here see us, give spirits water, make spirits speak. Is good blessing of spirits, is good blessing of man, is good every things. Me Kouamé Kpli from Krinjabo. My uncle him King-the Amon-Ndouffou. Him give me Nanan N'Verdjé. Nanan N'Verdjé him call me Eugène."

Eugène is not Cébon, but Kouamé Kpli, prince of Krinjabo, a personal gift from the king to Arthur Verdier. In the Bassamese tongue, Verdier is pronounced N'Verdjé. Eugène releases my hand, which is instantly grasped by another. One by one, all those present crush my fingers in greeting. As the Mandé-Dyula from the barracks step forward, amputation threatens. I am the centre of the compound. I have gone from curious to curiosity. The prince interrupts the procession of greetings; my hand is spared.

"Is news?"

I am being invited to talk about what has brought me here. I recount the night's events, the clamour of voices, the gunshot. Eugène is as attentive as a general listening to military dispatches. Hardly have I finished when he throws out a phrase to the assembled company. General laughter, a prince's gesture, silence.

"Adjo Blé, niece of me. Adjo Blé princess Krinjabo. White people very love Adjo Blé. All want Adjo Blé. But Adjo Blé not want white man. White always get problem with Adjo Blé. Always shouting, "Yubeech! Yubeech!" Adjo Blé have new name. Everyone say now Adjo Yubeech."

General laughter, a princely wave, silence.

"Dejean him fire gun at Adjo. Dejean bad man, not dangerous man. Dejean fire gun him miss pregnant hippopotamus in front him nose. Dejean very good at bad-temper. Adjo Yubeech her leave go sleep to Doctor Péan house. Here no more disturb her. Disturb doctor only."

General laughter, a princely wave, silence interrupted by the arrival of the trio Claude-Zéphirin-Ludovic.

"M'sieur Dabii! M'sieur Dabii! M'sieur Dabii!"

"You no stay here! You no stay here! You no stay here!"

"Bigboss Froucade him want you! Bigboss Froucade him want you! Bigboss Froucade him want you!"

Claude, Zéphirin, Ludovic . . . in that order, unless perhaps I have them the wrong way round. I send them back to Fourcade. I spend the whole afternoon in what, from the mess hall, looks like a courtyard, but from the ground level is clearly a princely court. At dinner that evening, the world is turned upside down. Doctor Péan delivers the customary compliment, but Eugène does not move. An awkward silence. Dejean smiles and takes over. Still Eugène does not move.

"Thank you for the meal, Eugène. Très bon!"

I mutter the words without looking up from my plate. Eugène takes his leave, Péan splutters, Dejean chokes, Fourcade drops his fork.

* * *

A letter from Assinie brings my time in Grand-Bassam to an end. Treich is ready to make a second exploration of the northern lands. Destination: Bondoukou and Kong country. Doctor Péan is concerned about the state of Treich's health and wants to check him over. We will make the journey together. Dejean and his Mandé-Dyula porters, Dreyfus and his rattling paraphernalia, set off some hours before us.

My last days in Grand-Bassam are spent in the court of Eugène Kouamé Kpli. He regales me with stories; whether they are myths or true accounts I do not know. Monsieur Verdier is granted the title Nanan, an honorific bestowed on men and women of high rank. Although the two are much the same age, Eugène talks of him like a father. I amuse him as I butcher the rudiments of Anyin that he teaches me. I am astounded by the progress he makes with the few French words and grammatical structures I teach him. On the day I am to leave, he demands a gift from me. I have nothing to give save a small box of tobacco. When I was leaving La Pallice, Amédée gave it to me when he entrusted me with a box for his friends in Assinie. Eugène disappears into his room to stow the box and returns with something more than a thank you: a smile.

"Here gift-one for you, Dabilly."

He extends his two empty hands and grips mine. I anticipate the crushing.

"This gift put safe in head! In Anyi, you not speak in day when shine sun-the. You wait for speak night-the. When you meet king-the, you not look in him eye. Look in eye of woman her beside king-the. When you him asking news, you raise flag. Safe in head, yes?"

The prince loosens his vice-like grip. He is kind enough to spare me a round of farewell handshakes. I leave, regretting that I haven't taught him that in French the article comes before the noun.

The Legend of the Dolphins, the Krumen and the Sandbar

Zibiyi was the most beautiful man in all creation. He was skilled at running, leaping, swimming, dancing, sculpting, fishing, ploughing; he could work as no man could. Seeing himself the object of great admiration, he became vain and impudent. He set out to seduce all women without exception. Having gone to the beach with Ziké, the young and beautiful wife of old Gougnon, the village féticheur or Kômian, Zibiyi plunged into the sea in order to amaze the maiden. A magical invocation and behold the insolent coxcomb condemned to frolic among the waves. Never to find the path back to shore. Ever since, his descendants come close to shore to show the beautiful Ziké how well they swim.

It was by watching the dolphins, the children of Zibiyi, that we, the Krumen, learned how to tame the sandbar. In a pirogue, you do not confront the wave. You cheat her. She races ever onward to the west, the shore. And so, when putting out, we sit four Krumen to starboard. From where she comes, she sees three and thinks there are but six oarsmen. On the voyage home, the oarsman changes side so that the wave will not discover the ruse. She is prideful and thinks to easily upturn the craft. She rolls gently while we row with all our might. *This is the moment when the arms sing, strong, pulsing and perfectly synchronised. The pirogue mounts the back of the "mother". No other wave dares block the path of the "mother". We allow ourselves to glide, proud sons of Zibiyi. None now control the vessel but the coxswain. He can set it down where he chooses.*

by James Clarck Vandernels Fredericssen de Oliveira Wayou

Master coxswain

Grand-Bassam

A TOUSLED BRAID
CHAPTER

ADJO Yubeech

From Grand-Bassam, due east, following the shoreline: Assinie. "Sun, no shade, sunstroke guaranteed. We shall march by night." Péan adopts the clipped tone of the veteran colonialist. Through the journey, neither he nor the waves fall silent. Clutching the belly of the clouds, a crescent moon sprawls on its back in a hammock of stars. Indolence, even in the heavens. In the moon's reflections, the sea is a cauldron of molten silver.

"There's been no France here since we were routed by the Germans. After the surrender, I worked in Iges, a filthy, squalid, military camp. I had just come down from medical school, but nothing that I learned there was of the least value. It was cauterise, amputate, cauterise, amputate, and wait for death to take them. Being a doctor there was as useful as being a cobbler in a country of legless men. All those dying, starving men trapped in an oxbow of the Meuse, humiliated by Prussian army rabble. Civilised in their own country, barbarous in ours. So many thousands of lives squandered, so much suffering for the vanity of Napoleon-the-third-toe and his cabal! Abandoning our African possessions to adventurers for such a thing – what a waste!"

Warily, I walk towards terra firma. Without shouting, Péan speaks over the crashing waves. The southerly wind from the sea carries his words. In the breeze, the white scarf around his neck frees itself and moves northwards like a compass needle. Walking on dry sand is difficult. Damp sand offers better support. As a wave recedes, we follow the ebb. As another approaches, we retreat. Given our trajectory, anyone following our tracks could imagine we were tipsy.

"Barter-based economics, treaty-based politics. A primitive model, but effective for the moment. When it comes to trade, we adopt Fourcade's formula: 'A good item for barter is cheap and tawdry in a gaudy or even outlandish container. Niggers favour crude, flashy colours and illustrations. The British quickly realised this.'"

He is using the word more frequently than usual. He may not be as centrist as I imagine. He imitates Fourcade all too well.

"When it comes to treaties, we follow Treich. With his jovial 'My deaaarest Anno', he has a way of winning the trust of the local chiefs. Last year, he brought back a dozen signed treaties, having left with a handful of infantrymen incapable of fending off a charging elephant."

I am less than reassured by the mention of a charging elephant. After all, this place is known as the Ivory Coast. Eugène tells us that pachyderms regularly come to the beach to bathe in the sea. After an hour's walk, I realise I have come further than I did in my solitary exploration to "Head in the

Water". The air is so heavy with salt it makes me thirsty. This time, at least, I have a canteen.

"There is no natural barrier separating us from the Gold Coast. It's the same country. Is there gold there? There's certainly gold here. Dreyfus is convinced we have discovered a new Transvaal. Especially since he heard about Assikasso, the 'land of gold' in Anyi. He swears there'll be a gold rush, like in the Klondike or South Africa. Officially, that canny old codger Verdier has played down the possible existence of gold. Unofficially, he has sent Dreyfus out to prospect. He constantly schemes to keep everything for himself. He wants to run the coast as a concession for ninety-nine years, the way Siiiir George Goldie does with his Royal Nigeeeer Company. For God's sake, we're not bloody Brits! This is France. Our enemy is not the Negro but the Englishman."

The moon has moved behind us. Further along the beach a shifting shadow is making a loud clatter. Crabs! Millions of crabs clicking their claws in a senseless dance. By day, they hide in holes, by night, they rule the shores. Beneath our feet, the sea of crabs parts without our crushing a single one. There is a rustle from the jungle. I am sure it is a herd of elephants. I forget all about the crabs, ready to dive into the sea. Doctor Péan, oblivious to my agitation, carries on his illustrious soliloquy.

"Verdier spent a long time on his own here. No regulations, no customs, no competition. What's more, Paris reimbursed him for every single investment he made on behalf of his company. His man Brétignière is a past master at dealing with the government. In these parts, a doctor of law is more useful than a medical doctor. He managed to secure compensation for the British blockade on Assinie despite the fact the wily old codger was trading with the Ashanti who were waging war on the Crown. Persuading perfidious Albion to pay for the very gunpowder we used to shoot them . . . Ah, Brétignière is a fine fellow, for all that, but a man of delicate health. On more than one occasion, we almost lost him. He looked very sickly when he came back. Before long, Paris will have the upper hand again. We shall have governors, administrators and civil servants running rampant. France is coming back and it will find me waiting. And since I am the most senior official, I shall soon be governor, my friend, governor!"

I cannot shake off the feeling of being spied on by a thousand eyes. I steel myself to this as our colonial march-cum-seminar continues. Péan speaks like a disillusioned man, worn down by a job he does not find fulfilling. In the mystic moonlight of the beach in the Gulf of Guinea, I find myself making excuses for him, until he comes to Dejean. He talks about Dejean the way people from Conty talk about those from Abilly, Parisians about people of Auvergne, or those from Poitiers talk about Corsicans or the Bretons: "Peasants, simple folk, parasites, hobgoblins, troglodytes, hayseeds, slobs, morons, an inferior race!" Their bucolic temperament and robust constitutions make people like Dejean better adapted to the noxious miasma of the tropics, while nobler, high-born souls are delicate, and must frequently return to the salutary air of the mother country to recover their strength. Although he has been here four years, Dejean has not suffered the slightest gastric trouble, the mildest fever, or even a hint of a bilious spell. Every day he bellows, blasphemes, swears, perjures, recriminates, incriminates, accuses, recuses, complains and curses his fate. No-one sees anyone but him, hears anyone but him. Far from the motherland, a race should be represented by the noblest branches of its family tree, not the stunted twigs. As far as Péan is concerned, Dejean is not a true White Man. It is an egregious historical error to allow Negroes to believe that Dejean represents the White Man.

In the celestial vault, those stars assigned to earth move in perfectly synchronised harmony. Ahead, the sun arches above the horizon. Behind, the moon dips its crescent into the salt sea. Day breaks, night ends. Only now do I notice that we are being followed. No, not the elephants. The thousands of eyes I conjured in the dark are merely two. A woman, coal-black skin, four tumbling, tousled braids, pointed breasts, scars shaped as stars around her navel. She is following our footsteps. As day breaks, Péan falls silent and once again becomes a doctor. He has known from the outset we are being shadowed by Adjo Yubeech.

* * *

Two days earlier, Dejean, Dreyfus and Bricard took a northernly route parallel to our own. By the time we arrive in Assinie, their cohort is camped outside Fort Joinville, a defensive bastion built on the site of the fort of Aniaba, true prince of France, false prince of Issiny. Already, Dejean is barking orders at a pair of porters while simultaneously hurling insults at the infantrymen and checking the contents of the bales with the jubilation of a Viking marauder. A myasthenic stone's throw away stands the home of the resident minister of France. Mounted on stilts, it has a whitewashed veranda that wraps around an upper floor beneath a thatched roof. Like all French buildings, it looks incongruous in this setting. A warm welcome. There are five of us on the veranda, half of the French population of a territory that stretches from Assinie to a latitude of 7°N. Treich is explaining, Dejean is complaining, Dreyfus is questioning, Péan is watchful, Bricard is taking notes. The resident of France is of above average height, with short hair, light-brown eyes and pleasing features. His almost feminine beauty is accentuated by the lack of a beard, although he sports moustaches in the fashion of the right bank of Châtellerault. He stands in the middle of the circle we have formed, hands in his jacket pockets, speaking slowly, looking at each of us in turn. I am gazing at the beach. In the early afternoon, shade is at a premium. Every living thing stands, sits or lies behind anything that might block the sun. Every living thing except her. She is staring at the sandbar. I can see her back.

"We have to forget the Portuguese model. River trade may have worked in the Americas, but it is impossible here. The draught is too shallow, the rapids too frequent, the natural obstacles too numerous; none of the rivers is navigable for any significant distance. The Comoé is navigable only as far as the village of Bettié. Chief Bénié Kwamin is well aware of the importance of his position on the northern route. By ransoming caravans, he is sending a message. I have managed to negotiate terms with all the chiefs except him. He is determined to raise the stakes."

With his reedy voice, haggard face, bilious expression and rasping breath, Treich is reminiscent of Amédée Brétignière. While he sets out his views, I scan the beach. Her back has found the shadow of a pirogue. Her hips sink into the sand.

"The Black chiefs are not the problem. They think that we are here merely to trade and are eager to make a profit. They are not yet aware that we plan to occupy the country. Right now, it is easier to get along with them than with the British. If they succeed in capturing Bondoukou and Kong to the north, all the caravans will be diverted to the Gold Coast, and Assinie and Grand-Bassam will be finished. Not simply as a French possession, but as trading posts."

Treich persuades by intelligence and force of character. His speech, in both form and content, is unlike anything I have ever heard. It is impossible to know on which side of the table he would be seated for Eugène's meals. The others listen more closely than I do. On the beach, the shadow of the pirogue contracts. The woman's back rises. The fine layer of sand clinging to her indigo-blue loincloth traces an apple over her buttocks. The back pats it with one hand, and the apple disappears in a shower of sand. The upper body swaying as she moves across the sand, the back walks towards a coconut tree, leans against it for a while, then once again sits down, head on its knees. The four tousled braids move in solidarity with the direction of her gaze. To left, to right, never towards the veranda.

"The new king of Krinjabo has told me that he will provide all necessary materials for us to push on as far as Kong if I so wish."

"Akassimadou is an inveterate liar. All he cares about is the gifts we shower on him, and an increase in our annual payments to him. That weakling could not so much as relieve himself in a bush without a battalion of féticheurs."

"For once, I agree with the pilferer of Negresses. Akassimadou is a rogue. His court is full of British spies."

Dejean and Péan are of one mind. A rare configuration, but the two have convergent interests. In order to take over the colony, they must first oust those loyal to Verdier. On the beach, the woman gets to her feet. A brief glimpse from the front, the pear-shaped breasts, the stars on her belly. And that pagne ... A few steps to the top of a dune, then she unties it and hunkers down, covering herself from head to toe. The pagne becomes a tent. A curious posture. As she stands up, the fabric glides down, ending its journey at the small of her back. With a quick movement, she adjusts it and the pagne is once again knotted about her rump. I scarcely have time to catch a glimpse of the red of her cache-sexe and a black curve of buttock. On the sand between her legs, a wet spot. She has just fashioned an improvised cloakroom on a beach teeming with fishermen, oarsmen, soldiers ...

Treich's voice rouses me from my stupor.

"You seem to know Krinjabo very well, my friends. But I place more trust in Akassimadou's lies than in your dealings with the dusky beauties of his court. I will keep the promise made by Verdier. I shall go to Bondoukou, then on to Kong to meet the famous LG. If he is still alive, as I believe, that is where I shall find him."

"In your condition, is it really wise to make such a perilous journey to look for a man who has already been posthumously promoted and decorated?"

"If I should disappear for a year and was rumoured to be dead, it would make me happy to think that one of you would move heaven and earth to give my mother and my sister definitive proof. Would you not feel likewise?"

For the first time since the start of the meeting, a silence settles over the veranda. On the beach, a man approaches the four tousled braids. Rather than chiding her for her shamelessness, as I anticipate, he curtsies. While I am puzzling over this, two other men run forward and grovel at her feet. Beneath the cloudy sky pierced by a blazing sun, a beach petrified by the heat, littered with pirogues, bristling with coconut palms, surmounted by a dune atop which stands a woman, almost as naked as an angel, with four tousled plaits, and half a dozen men at her feet ... A hackneyed scene becomes a baroque painting with tropical influences. Snatches of voices reach the veranda. I prick up my ears. Treich enters again.

"We shall leave Dreyfus with the gold panners of Akye. Dabilly will head up to the trading post at Assikasso. I will carry on to Bondoukou and, if all goes well, as far as Kong. To get home I have only to follow the Comoé."

"If you leave in your condition, nothing is certain. On your last expedition you almost died. The doctor in me insists that you rest a while. But the friend in me knows that you will not listen. And yet, you have men who can take on your duties. The Negroes have waited millennia for civilisation. They will survive a few more months."

"We do not have months, perhaps not even a week. The

future of these coastal lands as territories of France is being played out at this moment. Having routed the Ashanti and sacked their capital, Kumasi, the British have the advantage of terror."

"But that is what I am saying. We must send our most devious Senegalese infantrymen. The British do not play with tinpot Negro kings, they bring them to heel."

"You are wrong, Dejean. The British are enmeshed in a logic that can only bring defeat. Faced with their brutality, it will be easy for us to present ourselves as protectors. The Africans cannot know that we would never take up arms against the British. We have only to get there first and sign the treaties. The Berlin Convention and British fair play will do the rest. I leave as soon as possible."

"Who will govern in your absence?"

Dejean asks the question. Péan might just as well have asked it. On the dune, the men at the feet of the four tousled braids scatter.

"Bidaud, of course! Assisted by Chapper. With all the factories they have set up here, they know the locals well. I have written a letter to that effect to the lieutenant-governor in Dakar. I count on you, dear friend Péan, to send it by the next French cargo ship. Above all, do not send it by telegraph. The British control the lines. Let us not divulge our intentions. And tell Bidaud to come and see to things here. He is in Alépé."

Dejean's disappointment is tempered by the fact that Péan has not been promoted in his place. And vice versa. To judge by his expression, the doctor is the more humiliated. Bidaud and Chapper are Verdier men, pillars of the CFK. Like Péan's mirage, the tableau on the beach has dissolved. She is once again alone, standing at the foot of the coconut tree, staring at the waves. Aside from a handful of Mandé-Dyulas who hail from lands where the stormiest waves are splashes in a bathtub, I have never seen anyone admire the sea simply for the beauty of the spectacle. As the sun declines, her shadow and that of the coconut tree extend. The twin ghosts vie with each other in elegance. She moves, the tree remains rooted. All honours to the moving image that I follow with my eyes.

The conference on the veranda concludes with the Apéritif de France, the new colonial fashion, a bitter alcoholic drink that allegedly contains quinine. Dejean and Péan are the first to leave the Residence. Doubtless promoted by disappointment. Dreyfus, with an air of mild euphoria, shows off some gold-bearing nuggets brought back from the Klondike. He compares them to nuggets from the territories of Anyi and Attié. His needlessly abstruse presentation is supposed to help us understand the troubling similarities between geological layers separated by thousands of kilometres. His erudition is wearying. Fortunately, mosquitoes prompt a hasty departure to the house where he has taken up residence. Bricard disappears without warning. I alone remain.

Tasselled sailor's hat, pipe clenched between his teeth, checked shirt, pagne tied about his waist, and walking shoes, a Black man with the air of a Scottish laird appears. His androgynous features are disconcerting in a man with such a strong, muscular frame. Any confusion is further heightened by his sonorous voice, as he speaks in a refined, unaccented French.

"Would the gentlemen care for another aperitif?"

He drinks from an imaginary glass, exaggerating the grimace of someone encountering the bitter beverage. Treich introduces me: Louis Anno, his interpreter. They greet each other warmly and talk as though I were not here. They are not entirely mistaken. The beach glows in the red rays of the dying sun. I look about vainly but she is nowhere to be seen. Adjo Yubeech has disappeared.

*　*　*

The night is young. We light a bonfire beneath the veranda, part illumination, part mosquito repellent. Back in La Rochelle, Amédée gave me not only a cardboard box, but an oral message. He insisted that I deliver it only in the presence of Treich and Anno. They now sit facing me. "*Ndè-ndé ndè-ndé sou ba!*" I learned my first Anyi phrase in the offices of Amédée Brétignière. It is one I have repeated dozens of times. Even when sick to my stomach aboard the *America*. The delivery of my message divides opinion. Treich's expression darkens, while the androgynous Anno talks to me.

"Kouamé Kpli says that you are the fastest learner of Anyi he has ever met."

"Eugène is a patient teacher. How did you know?"

"Here, anything that matters is quickly known. Never forget that. Giving bed and board to any passing stranger is not just traditional hospitality. Asking them for news from where they began their journey is not just a polite protocol. Hospitality is an intelligence service. Now, tell us what Brétignière's message means?"

"*Ndè-ndé* means 'quickly', *ndè-ndé ndè-ndé* probably means 'very quickly'. *Ba* means 'to come'. Put together they mean 'someone or something is coming very quickly.'"

"That's fine, but we are no further advanced. We need to interpret, not translate."

"Like Saint-Pierre."

We all laugh. The playful tone conjures the image of Adjo. Why did she follow us? On whose behalf? I imagine her at Fort Joinville in the company of a Péan who ignores her, a Bricard who pursues her or a Dejean who threatens her. I have seen so little of her, know so little of her and the urge to protect her leaves me utterly helpless. Now plunged into darkness, the beach offers only a glint of the white ribbon of wave foam. My visions of Adjo Yubeech dissolve in the erudite company of these two men who share the intimacy of lovers. They force me out of the two-toned vision, the general binary of these climes. Black/white, France/Britain, state/company – there is none of that on the veranda. Two partners entertain a guest. True. Anno speaks. For the first time today, a conversation captures my full attention.

"Surprising as it may seem, Saint-Pierre is an excellent interpreter. Without opening his mouth, he can make himself understood in any part of this country. Words are singular, gestures are universal. What needs to be interpreted in this sentence is what it does *not* say. *Ndè-ndé ndè-ndé is* typical Brétignière. Back on the Élima plantation, he would urge the workers on, bellowing 'Vite! Vite!' But now he's ill and he knows he will not recover. Like an Anyi chieftain, he has chosen where he will die. He is coming back. I do not even have to open the box he gave you to give to us to know what is inside."

"What is it?"

"Nothing. It is physically empty, but spiritually full. Amédée has entrusted you with a fragment of his soul to tell us how much his body has grown lighter."

"Anno, stop upsetting our guest. He has other preoccupations. It is time to show him to his quarters."

The two friends exchange a smile. Anno leads me to a door, bids me goodnight, then fades into the darkness. My room at the Résidence de France is identical to the one at Fort Verdier. The wick of an oil lamp, buffeted by the breeze, illumines it with a dancing flame. Curled up in a corner on the floor lies a figure. Four tousled braids tumble from the head.

A HEADS-HELD-HIGH CHAPTER

REVOLUTIONARY CLASS

A lot of the ladies wear their hair in braids like sea urchins, like Maman sometimes does. I put my hand on the fat bottom of a lady in a long dress trailing on the ground. She gives me evil looks, but at least I know she doesn't have a hidden tail. I ask the men to take off their hats to check they don't have horns. From a distance, I think I see a wolf's fangs in the mouth of a yawning man. Up close, I see it's because the man has only two teeth in his head. Lots of waving hands. I stare at them intentively. There are some long painted nails, especially on the women, but no claws. As for the colonial hell, Comrade Papa was all present and correct: no devil, just the heat. A doctor with a torch looks in my mouth for yellow fever, then listens to my heart using my favourite French word: "stethoscope". He doesn't find anything because he's looking for the wrong colour fever. Mine is the red fever of the struggling masses. I'm pushed through a door into a huge hall filled to the brim with working-class zeal. Shouts, laughs, leaps, hugs, scenes of fraternisation. It's just like *The Big Night* but in the middle of the day. Sitting on the suitcase

113

containing all my foreign affairs, I watch the spectacle of happy people. Above my head, a very large poster is hanging from the ceiling for all to see. The man in the photo looking down on the working-class zeal looks like he's descending from the clouds like Comrade Hodja in Mama's Albanianist paradise.

His Excellency The President of the Republic: printed letters made to look like writing. When the people are governed by an *Excellency*, they're weighed down by a medi-evil yolk. When they're ruled by a *Monsieur-le-Président*, they're sub-servants to the bossy bourgeoisie. That must mean that the proletariat here are sub-servants to medi-evil bourgeois yolk. So why is there all this working-class zeal in the hall? I take out my book of revolutionary notes for Comrade Papa. I write lots of stuff, I have a lot of time. There's no-one here to pick me up. Right under the poster of the evil bourgeois yolk, I see a revolutionary clue: from inside the red-light window of a smooch-seller, Amédée Pierre is watching the working class from dozens of record sleeves playing 33 rpm in a music shop. When it gets to midnight, everyone has left and the arrivals hall is almost empty. I'm tired, I'm sleepy and I'm hungry, but I'm standing firm. Every now and then I get asked where my parents are by someone or other. Probably spies for the evil bourgeois yolk on the poster dangling from the ceiling. I don't tell them anything. I'm on my guard. People start to notice me because now the hall is like an African desert. There's suspicious goings-on behind the Air France kiosk. The reactionary forces launch an assault. In a two-pronged attack they try a pincer movement to surround me. One of them smiles, a class traitor. The other is a brute with a horrible face. I carefully hide my revolutionary notepad under my shirt.

"Little white boy, you here alone many hours still. You very hungry, no? Come, we get you some eat then find your parents."

An attempt to corrupt a revolutionary agent on a mission. I won't say a word, not even if they put me up against the cemetery wall of Pear-Lash-ays. Stand firm and resist. I hug my rucksack to my tummy. The reactionary forces are closing in. Escape manoeuvre. I try to run for it but I trip and fall. The grew-some brute grabs me.

In the office for the oppression of the sovereign people, the food the class traitor gives me is really weird, like nothing I've ever seen before. A white ball and small bits of meat swim in a thick soup with a colour somewhere between revolutionary red and coward's yellow. I'm afraid of poison, but some of the sauce is deepest red. And anyway, you can't go around doing a dictatorship of the proletariat on an empty stomach. I dive into the suspicious dish, gobbling it up in less time than it takes Comrade Papa to set the inexorable march of progress in motion. The brute whistles through his teeth. The class traitor hands me a bottle of Coke. I jerk back, although I'm not surprised by this underhand tactic. They begin the three degrees. They know I've come from Amsterdam via the Paris Commune. My papers were in the neck bag which is now in the hands of the class traitor. "Ilitch"? I don't react. "Davidovitch?" Silence. "Shaoshan?" Silence. I only answer to Maman's name, the one that never seems to fit when we write down all the names that Comrade Papa gave me. But they don't know that.

The thug doesn't take his eyes off me. The class traitor never lets me out of his sight. He's talking non-stop. It's not the exact same language Comrade Papa talks, but I understand. The sentences are shorter and there's bits missing all over the place. Actually, it's a lot easier to understand. The telephone in the office for the oppression of the sovereign people rings. The thug jumps, he's surprised. It's really funny. Inside my head, I tell the phone to ring again. And it does. And every time, the big brute jumps. I laugh. They like it when I laugh. With every *ring-ring*, the thug jumps higher and I laugh harder and they laugh too. The forces of oppression don't seem so bad. I decide to talk.

"Tremble with fear, pawns of mindless stateless capitalism, shiver with cold! The dictatorship of the proletariat is on the march, the workers' revolution is at hand to mouth. Down with the reactionary medi-evil bourgeoisie . . . Down with the aristocracy! Long live the revolution! Long live the sovereign people!"

At home, in front of the mirror, I don't sound too convincing. But here, in the face of the reactionary forces, with my fist raised and the opium of the people in my voice, I know Comrade Papa would be proud. The thug and the class traitor freeze. Then lots of laughing and slapping: they're laughing so hard I think they might explode and they're slapping their bellies at the same time.

The henchman and the class traitor take me around lots of offices in the airport. It's really weird being in a country where everyone's from the Boni-Marron tribe. But the people here have a serious problem working out colours and sizes. They call me "little white boy". Maybe this is a sign of the alien nation Comrade Papa talks about. I'm not small and I'm not white. They track down my uncle and aunt, who are supposed to come and pick me up. While I'm waiting for them to arrive, lots of men and women and other reactionary forces come in to listen to me talk about the workers' revolution. They laugh and smile with their big white teeth. The henchman and the class traitor are my ministers of propaganda. They bring people in to listen to me. I speechify like Comrade Papa about the revolution and the lost chains.

Émile and Geneviève show up when I'm in the middle of the international conspiracy against Lumumba the travelling beer salesman. They're the aunt and uncle who were supposed to come and pick me up. The class traitor and propaganda minister walk me out to Émile's car. It's a Fiat 127, with the big "F" for fascist in the logo and a brownshirt on the side. What is that doing here? I shout about how Fiat cars are made from the sweat of working-class brows on the bent backs of the labouring masses to enrich an Italian family who were dirty collaborators just like the Philips in the Netherlands. I don't even have time to talk about Volkswagen, the People's Car that was propriated by a different crazy Adolph and his gang of swas-stickers. Émile shoves me into the car under the sun. Actually, I'm pretty happy because I've never been inside a car before. In our red-light district of De Wallen, I sometimes use Comrade Papa's little red bicycle, and sometimes sit behind Maman on her Soviet socialist motorbike, but mostly I use the working-class public transport. I've only taken private transport one time. When Yolanda gave me a piggyback. There's a picture pinned to the door of the fall-back camp latrine of me as a baby, in a coloured pagne, slung across the big bum of Yolanda, who is laughing with her big white teeth. Comrade Papa, who's always serious, is jabbing his fist at the camera on account of workers' rights and employers. Maman's there but she's not there because she's the one taking the picture.

* * *

Bridge, lagoon, a few buildings, then jungle, jungle, jungle ... The landscape flashing past is as strange as the food I got from the class traitor. The road snakes its way through the inexplicable forest. From a distance, it looks like the trees are cutting it off. Up close, they leave a tunnel of green for the brown-shirted car. The only forest I've ever seen is in the park that I sometimes go to with Maman on her Soviet socialist moped, a red Vespa made of sheet metal, with wheels and exhaust pipes from world war bombers that have no business being in the air in peacetime. According to Maman, tanks should be turned into tractors, swords into plough shares, anti-tank batteries into AA batteries, mortars into cement, three-star generals into five-star engineers, and lots of other war things into peace things. We have to put all the trap things of war into the hands of the revolutionary workers and the peasants so they can make the bourgeois capitalist bend down. Those who aren't flexible enough are given public executions, according to Comrade Papa, or they get put up against the wall. Maman and Comrade Papa are always in two minds about stuff. This is good for the cries of the sovereign people on the rare occasions when they're together. The forest in my local park is very neat with straight lines of trees and big wide paths. If Maman isn't too tired, we play hide-and-seek and we always find each other. But Maman would never find me in this huge forest like the jungle of the Boni-Marrons in Suriname. Yolanda is the only person who could find me.

In the fascist Fiat on the black tarmac snaking through the middle of the forest, Émile grumps and grouches about Comrade Papa. He wants him to stop wanting to change the world and change himself instead. He probably doesn't know that Comrade Papa has so many Mao shirts that he could give one to everyone in the whole world. Émile says that you can't raise a child the way you train a monkey. Émile can't understand why Comrade Papa didn't tell them exactly when I was arriving. But I know. It was a diversionary tactic. But I don't say nothing. Geneviève talks about Maman with her heart on her short sleeves and a kindness in her voice. She says that I look a lot like Maman. That we have the same eyes. That I'm white, like her. She's half right. People always say that I've got Maman's eyes. But like all the other people here, Geneviève has a serious problem with colours. She's even got plans to paint me. She says that if I painted my face dark black, I'd look just like someone called Nanan Alloua-Treissy. Geneviève has another big problem. Every time our long march through the forest is interrupted by a few houses, she calls it a town. Even I know that towns can't be that small. But I don't say anything. After a few hours in the fascist car, the sun starts to play hide-and-seek behind the trees of the impenetrable forest. Eventually it disappears and everything is pitch black. There's nothing to see. Émile and Geneviève silently say nothing.

119

There's nothing more to hear. Having spent two revolutionary days holding forth and fifth about leaders even more maximal than Comrade Fidel Cuban Cigar, I sleep. I can't remember getting to Assikasso.

Émile is a peasant chocolate farmer. He plants the cocoa trees that grow the chocolates. Geneviève is a minor schoolteacher. She teaches at EPP Assikasso 2 State School for Minors. The school is so big that Comrade Papa could organise all the working-class meetings he dreams about. The playground is right under the big blue sky. Not like the little yard at my old school behind the walls of the Oude Kerk. Actually, EPP Assikasso 2 is so huge that all the teachers and their families live inside. They live in little houses with gardens full of tulips, the same flowers that kicked off the stalk exchange and capitalist oppression. Émile and Geneviève don't have any children. Even here, I'm an only child, I float around the outer space of a big bedroom all to myself like Comrade Cosmonaut Yuri Gagarin in the Vostok. You could fit two of our old apartments in here, including the re-education camp. The first night in the bedroom, I can't get back to the sleep I started in the car, I have too many things to think. Next morning, since we live inside the school, I'm taken to class by hand. Geneviève grabs my hand and drags me there. I try to put on the brakes on account of I still want to sleep. And also cos I'm scared. When she gets to the classroom with me in tow, the children stand up as one man and shout:

"Good morrrrrrning, maaaadame!"

I ease off the brake, and we go into the classroom. The boys all look identically the same with beige shorts and shirts and plastic shoes. The girls are all twins in their blue-and-white checked pinafores and leather shoes. Very disciplined! Even their heads all have the same black frizzy hair. With my rusty frizzless red hair, I'm going to be the outsider again. The boys are all so tall that Moody Marko would feel like a midget. Some of the girls have got gentlemen's all-sorts, but they're a lot smaller than Yolanda's. The schoolmaster smiles at Geneviève and then he says:

"Now, class, we've got a new pupil today."

"Good morrrrrrning, camaraaaade!"

I think maybe I'm still dreaming in the sleep I didn't get to finish. A genuine revolutionary class! This isn't something out of Comrade Papa's books and speeches. It's a real working-class class. I sit up straight in the legal revolutionary attitude. The schoolmaster says:

"Say good morning to the class."

Arms by my sides like a capital "I", I tap the ground with my right heel and swivel on my left heel. A perfectly executed left quarter-turn towards the class. My voice is clear and resolute.

"Good morning, fellow-comrades. Long live the revolution!"

Obviously, I have one fist raised; Geneviève puts both hands on her head. The teacher waves her away. As soon as she walks out the door, the class sits down as one man. Revolutionary discipline. For the first time ever, no-one is looking at me, not even out of curiosity. A girl sitting right in front of the teacher's desk moves over on her bench and I sit down. The girl raises her head and so does the whole class. It looks like the Great Helmsman is going to speak. I look at the teacher, who's standing with his back to the class. He raises his head. I decide to do like everyone else. I'm more confused than the first time I got lost at Amsterdam Centraal. My new working-class class is truly revolutionary. Above the blackboard is a television and it's switched on.

The Legend of the Pact of Ahounyanssou

We lived along the banks of a river that provided water and enriched our lands with silt so fecund that we did not have to bend in order to grow food. Éhuia-Râ, the sun god, shed his glittering rays upon the gold we took from the riverbed. Toutou Aka-Amon, Aké-Naton, Râm'ssèssè, Amon-Otèp, Amon-Éfhui, Amon-Amath, N'séti, N'néfertiti, Asan-ti, Opokoun-ti: our kings and queens were garlanded with precious metals. For them, our scholars designed opulent palaces which were built by the sweat and toil of the countless peoples we enslaved. When they died, we interred them in edifices vast enough to contain riches and companions so that they should want for nothing in the land-hereafter, where life is longer than it is on earth. But, blinded by the vanity of glistering gold, each ruler demanded a vaster and more lavish sepulchre than his predecessor. So preoccupied were we with constructing and embellishing these tombs that we did not anticipate the incursions from the savages of Hélâ-Assi to the north, the beasts of Ama-Assi to the west, the vandals of Ass-iria to the east. We remained in the south. Following the riverbanks, we fled. When we passed the village of Nanan Assa-wan, we scattered, the better to elude the enemy *pursuing us. Some headed due west towards Kokoli-Kongo. Some scaled the high plateaus with Nana Niti'opia. We fled south-west, through the boundless lands of sand: Ahounyanssou.*

Ahounyanssou is an arid desert where rolling dunes extend as far as the eye can see. We knew how to survive. He who would seek gold must first find water. The enslaved peoples knew this and did not perish. After a long crossing, they halted when they came to the first stand of trees. We named the land Aféli-Kongo, the land of the weary. We gave them back their freedom and assigned to them the warlord, Kakou Mensah, to protect them and to cover our retreat. They pledged undying loyalty: the pact of Ahounyanssou. Even today, they refer to their kings as Mensah. We carried on our way to lands that were rich in gold. In memory of ancient times, we settle near a river and continue to leave an empty square at the centre of our villages. We still entomb our kings with all their gold but accompanied by only a few house slaves known as kangah. The age of pyramids is over!

> *Kouamé Kpli Eugène Cébon*
> *Maître d'hôtel at Fort Verdier*
> *Grand-Bassam*

A MANTICORE CHAPTER

MALAN ALLOUA

A white man, alone deep in uncharted territory, in the dark heart of impenetrable jungle, fettered by the tangled snarl of liana, machete in hand, rifle slung over his shoulder, battling the raging elements, prey to wild beasts unknown to even the most learned naturalists, at the mercy of the cruel anthropophagous peoples . . . but a man who proceeds without fear, guided by the spirit of his race, ennobled by his sense of duty, elevated by the abiding interest of civilisation . . . Books, newspapers and magazines, chronicle and pamphlets all serve to mould a collective imagination in which the Explorer, custodian of the highest moral values, magnifies both the limits of courage and the boundaries of empire. In this, true heroes like Stanley, Livingstone and de Brazza are paragons.

Along this jungle path, the morning caravanserai sets off, clumsy, raucous and chaotic, giving the lie to this idyllic image. The vanguard is led by the standard-bearer, Anyi Tano, followed by three interpreters, including Louis Anno, who is travelling with his two wives, four children and two maids; some fifteen infantrymen from Fort Joinville militia in mismatched uniforms, bayonets attached to their Chassepots, trailed by a similar number of women, some with children strapped to their backs, carrying crates of ammunition, kitchen utensils and sundry other bundles balanced on their heads; a team of porters numbering thirty-two lanky Mandé-Dyulas and a dozen squat, muscular Akapless, stoically bearing the weight of Dejean's trunk and Dreyfus's boxes; six "boys" whose role is to serve the three white men; and two goats pulled along by a dozen unidentified attendants. Plus Adjo, my room-mate, like a Greek oracle, covered from head to toe in a suit of white linen. The caravan extends for almost fifty metres. As it advances, so the distance between the two groups increases. After a two-hour march, Treich, Dreyfus, Anno and I leave the group. A side track leads down to a makeshift landing stage on the banks of a lagoon. Le Voaz, the captain of the *Diamant*, is waiting for us. We are using this lagoon steamer converted into a gunboat to transport much of our food and the various belongings for which we do not have porters. We glide across the Abi, a large inland lake to the north of Assinie. It is ringed by a curtain of lush green. There are no banks or shores. The forest tumbles down the steep slopes to the water's edge. The hundred and fifty acres that make up the Compagnie de Kong coffee plantation cling to one such slope, near the village of Élima.

The *Diamant* heads due north. It is equipped with a 52 mm gun, a Hotchkiss machine gun and twelve Czech repeating rifles called Kropatcheks in the hands of Senegalese infantrymen. Even without the Lebels made by my friends in Alsace, the steamer's arsenal means that it has unrivalled firepower on all navigable waters, coastal and inland. Numerous mutinous or rebellious villages have already tasted its lead. Some years ago, following an unfortunate misunderstanding about the sad fate of one Captain Thévenard, the *Diamant* attacked Abi, the village which gave its name to the lagoon. The offensive lasted only one morning; Abi was razed to the ground. When peace was restored, the village chief asked the meaning of the sign painted on the hull of the gunboat. Louis Anno said that the interpreter found it all but impossible to convince the good man that diamonds were stones used to make precious jewellery for the women of France. "Now I understand why the White Man travels alone," Chief Amon d'Abi is said to have concluded. "The White Woman must be truly fearsome." The telling of a story is the beginning of a lesson. This is something that I learned from Eugène. I'm waiting for the lesson Anno will deliver, as he leans on the gunwale of the *Diamant*.

"In these lands, there is no Penelope. A wife does not wait at home, she travels with Odysseus. The young lady from the other night . . ."

"Nothing happened."

"I do not for a moment doubt your chivalrous nature. It is entirely to your credit that nothing happened. And honour is the quality that Anyi women find most seductive. Did you not notice that, this morning, she was completely covered?"

"I did."

"And you noticed that she was swathed all in white?"

"Yes."

"She is proclaiming to all who wish to hear that her womb has been inviolate since birth, that she is a woman of honour and that she has made her choice. And I think there is no mystery as to the chosen one, Mes'sieur Dabilly."

"..."

"Our first stop, Krinjabo, is her home village. There, she is a highly important person, and not simply because she is a member of the royal household. But I think she plans to travel further with us; with you."

A Black interpreter with an androgynous face sporting a sailor's hat with a red pompom starts to babble about some Black Eve with tousled braids and stars scarred on her belly aboard a jury-rigged steamer armed like a British fortress that crests the waves of an inland sea encircled by vegetation as old as Adam. The image cloaks me in a cloud of fantasy. "Here we are!" Treich barks, bringing me back to reality. At the far end of a bay, the River Bia cascades into the Abi lagoon down steep rapids blocked by boulders. The sailing ends, back to dry land. A kilometre's walk and we reach Krinjabo, capital of the Anyi kingdom of Sanwi.

* * *

Our flag flutters from one of the branches of the Krinja, the village's emblematic ficus, which struggles to shade the central square. Treich is calm, Dreyfus excitable. Doubtless at the sight of the men and women of the royal court bedecked in gold. If a celestial metalsmith should chance to pass through the main square of Krinjabo to his foundry, he would encounter a shimmering pool of gold. Fingers, toes, wrists, ankles, ears, necks, noses, the handles of canes and fly whisks ... everything is pierced, inlaid or shrouded in gold. Were it not for this, the royal court would look like a circus troupe, a motley group of characters dressed in fineries found in a dusty attic. Flamboyant umbrellas, musketeer's rapiers; pocket watches hung around necks; constellations of medals including the Légion d'honneur and the Mérite agricole pinned to loin-cloths, tunics, anywhere; pince-nez dangling from ears; paper parasols painted with Chinese ideograms; vestments embroi-dered with cabalistic signs; a surgeon's apron; a spyglass with no lens; threadbare tailcoats; and sundry objects as likely to be found in these parts as a Black man serving as adviser to George Washington. The prize for the truly unexpected goes to the millinery. Eugène Cébon is not the only man to favour the Phrygian cap; it adorns the head of every other notable. There are a number of bowler hats, a scattering of tricorns, three tarbooshes, a Pickelhaube and an opera hat that, at the slightest movement of its wearer, wiggles on its broken spring. But despite their iconoclastic attire, the members of court are marked by a noble bearing and graceful posture, imbued with the hauteur common to royal courts around the world.

The main square is surrounded by the common people. We are seated on one side, King Akassimadou and his court on the other. Louis Anno stands between the rival camps. The impression is one of gladiators preparing to do battle. Silence adds to the tension. His august posterior enthroned upon a genuine rickety Louis XIV chair upholstered in British fabrics, the king is dressed in a brightly coloured Spahi officer's jacket that is much too small and has lost all its buttons. Surprising though it might seem, he wears the corresponding pale blue képi. An attendant holds a parasol above his head, moving it up and down to make the golden tassels dance. To his right, a lackey waves a fan of ostrich feathers. To his left sits a white woman, daubed from head to foot with the milky clay called kaolin. A pristine pagne is tied about her waist, her breasts sag to her stomach, her face is stone, her eyes fixed, unblinking: a living statue seated on a stool of solid gold.

A public exchange of gifts. It is important that the crowd witness France's generosity and its respect for Akassimadou's power. Then, an exchange of words. Treich speaks, Anno echoes, the staff-bearer whispers into the king's ear. Each reply makes the return journey. The king never speaks in public. The staff-bearer is master of ceremonies. Dressed only in a simple pagne, he and his sober attire contrast sharply with the rest of the court. And as his name suggests, wherever the king goes, he carries the staff. After the requisite expression of gratitude, platitudes about each other's health, observations about the meteorological considerations, the dangers of the jungle, the vicissitudes of the travel and so on, Treich introduces Dreyfus as a scientist sent by Verdier to study the secrets of the soil's fecundity. Someone wishes him luck in finding the earth's testicles. The crowd bursts out laughing. Treich waits for this to subside before introducing me as an envoy of Amédée Brétignière. A few heads nod at the mention of the man who spent years travelling through these lands. Then the purpose of the trip is explained: Bondoukou, Kong, the search for our compatriot LG, and, above all, the threat posed by the British. No bureaucratic patter, no asides. I am astounded by the fact that this discussion is taking place in public, witnessed and judged by the *vulgum pecus*. I cannot believe that this is protocol. A man of power, wherever his kingdom, whatever his colour, cannot risk discussing affairs of state before his subjects. To weigh the merits of an issue without appearing to do so. Akassimadou is playing a power game. He pretends not to remember the treaty signed by his uncle. Nevertheless, in the name of his friendship with Verdier, he agrees to help. He will provide porters, food, interpreters and blessings to ensure that Treich's venture is a success. His public statement is in no way binding. What matters is what he says during the secret negotiations. But these formal expressions of fellow feeling from France have brought him prestige in the eyes of his people.

After an hour of palaver that is of no interest to us, the crowd becomes restless and distracted, which signals the end of the session. Even the novelty of seeing white men has its limits. Then the white woman, the kaolin statue with the face of stone, comes to life. She makes a discreet wave and silence falls like a cloak over the assembled company. Her voice is guttural, her lips barely moving. The staff-bearer cranes to make out what is being said. She is staring at me. I cannot believe that this creature is speaking to me. Her words make the journey through the staff-bearer and the interpreter. Louis turns to me. I have to face it, this creature is addressing me. Louis can sense my self-consciousness. He answers directly, in other words, he speaks on my behalf. The guttural voice cuts him short. The staff-bearer withdraws. The crowd is silent. We can hear the air quiver. Anno steps forward, I cut him short. The interpreter withdraws. I know what the white woman wants of me: the lessons learned from Eugène Cébon, stage one.

"I am Maxime Dabilly, son of Pierre Dabilly and Catherine Bernard. My grandfather was a soldier who was rewarded for his bravery in battle with a plot of land that bears his name. I come to offer greetings from my little village in France, where the name Krinjabo came from. The news I bring is good; no tragedy has brought me here. My mouth is full of words, but the word that commands is 'albino'. It is white with truth and cannot endure the sun's glare."

Eugène calls this "raising a flag": a public pronouncement of one's name, lineage and origins. In Krinjabo, as in Abilly, to have a name means to have parents and land. The idea of the Explorer is a European myth. There is no scrap of land that has not been claimed by a human being. You have discovered nothing; you have arrived uninvited. When you meet others, you tell them who you are. "Hello, my name is . . ." The first part of my speech in Anyi was easy to learn. More difficult to memorise was the cryptic formula about the word albino, which signifies that important subjects should not be discussed in public. Speaking a language that I do not understand is something I have known for a long time. There are murmurs from the audience. Barely audible at first. Then, I hear the word "Parisian". Another call of "Parisian!" And another . . . With the speed of a powder trail, the square begins to erupts with calls of "Parisian! Parisian!" I fear a riot but am reassured by Louis Anno's smile. "Parisian! Parisian!" The staff-bearer attempts to restore calm. To no avail. He adjourns the meeting amid the deafening cacophony. "Parisian! Parisian!" The royal court disperses. The crowd falls on me. It takes all the might of our Senegalese infantrymen to deliver me from the enthusiastic mob.

* * *

The village of Krinjabo lies in a clearing the shape of a haricot bean. We have pitched camp on the western edge. No man has been lost. Yet. In the jungle, a caravanserai is not merely a procession of equidistant members moving at a uniform speed. Sometimes it can take several days to reassemble the team. Desertions occur, but they are rare. Transporting men, food, weapons and equipment is a job like any other, one that fosters esprit de corps: travelling in all weathers, along paths that even the hardiest beasts of burden will not take, the porters are the heroes of our jungle expeditions. One night, Schäkele reads us an article in which Stanley pays tribute to them. Somewhat unexpected given the man's reputation for consummate immorality. Porters are indispensable because there are no carts. In the jungle, horses and donkeys are laid waste by humidity and disease. Introduce camels? Impossible. None of these animals could withstand the humidity for more than a week. Create roads? With all these towering trees, such a task would require a half-breed born of Titan and Sisyphus. Left untravelled for only a few days, and nature reasserts itself.

At the Krinjabo bivouac, all our porters are present and correct. Thanks to my success this afternoon, we have recruited some new faces. The gifts from the royal household consist of a procession of domesticated animals, including six goats. On one of these, we feast. The Senegalese infantrymen and the Mandé-Dyula porters roast it on skewers. They celebrate to the rhythms of the polytonal tambourines wedged under their armpits. Their songs waft through the air with the mouth-watering aromas. Anyi porters and their kin gather for the traditional Anno family stew. Head, neck, ribs, tripe, giblets, feet and sundry bony parts: they believe that the prime cuts should be boiled into soups so heavily spiced as to be criminal. On a three-month excursion, transporting the canned food and drinks for a single white man would require a dozen porters. Aside from slowing any progress, the resulting costs would be much higher. Thus, the profitability and efficacy of colonial expeditions depend on eating locally, by which I mean the ability to tolerate chilli in such lethal doses. You should see Treich feasting on Mrs Anno's stewed offal! I do not dare. Tonight, I shall dine on Senegalese infantrymen's brochette, served with boiled yams and a red drizzle of palm oil.

Once dinner is over, there is a staff meeting. Notes from Treich's previous expedition have enabled the Topographical Society of France to create a more accurate map of the region, which is now spread out before our grave faces. Treich indicates points and lines that make as much sense to me as a Zulu translation of the Holy Missal. He plots and re-plots our itinerary several times. He is hesitant. Heading due north would follow the course of his earlier expedition. There are several staging points along the way, and at each it is important to stop and check that the French flag is still flying over the places where treaties were signed.

"I said I would come back bearing gifts. Nothing pleases an African chieftain more than a promise kept. Each stop will require days of parleys and celebrations. But the journey is shorter—"

"And the route more difficult, my friend," Anno interrupts. "A ten-day trek across hilly terrain. In the tropical forest, a small hill is the equivalent of a mountain back home. The slopes are steep, muddy and covered with a thick tangle of vegetation. If you don't break your neck on going up or down, you have to avoid being drowned in the stream at the foot of every hill. And the slightest drizzle anywhere upstream can turn the smallest brook into a biblical flood. First scale the mountains, then part the waters ... Given your state of health, my friend, you would be ill-advised to play Moses of the Anyi lands several times a day."

The bowl of Anno's pipe glows as he inhales. A whorl of smoke escapes his nostrils. No-one really knows where he learned the language of the préfet and the manners of a viscount. The north-north-west route on Treich's map joins the left bank of the Comoé near Yakassé. It would entail venturing into the unknown, but the certainty of a less arduous route since the path alongside a river is flat. Travelling inland by following rivers is something of a French speciality. Whether along the Mississippi and the Saint Lawrence in the Americas; along the Mekong and the Yangtze in Cochinchina and Indochina; along the Senegal and Niger in West Africa; along the Ogooué and the Congo in equatorial Africa; the Ubangi and Chari in central Africa; or the Rhône, Rhine, Loire and Garonne, France has followed rivers for centuries. Man does not change, even when he is expanding his empire. At the far end of the scale, the British travel straight as the crow flies. An island nation, accustomed to cramped conditions, they are parsimonious in their choice of routes. Their philosophy of occupation can be summed up by taking the shortest, most practical route. So, do we travel in the British fashion or the French? The problem of choosing a route has not been resolved when the heralds of His Majesty King Akassimadou are announced.

* * *

The bustling village of early afternoon is now ghostly. Standing in the main square, the Krinja tree looks like a succubus. A colony of bats flutters in its branches, their calls merely adding to the gloom. The Anyi people say these messengers of lost souls speak so they may see, and, if they are silent, they are lost. Our escorts are silent, but they are not lost. With the keen night vision of bats, they guide us through the warren of alleys that wind between the huts. A perimeter wall, an inner court-yard, bodies lying on the ground. Stumbling at times, we step over them, but they do not move. Are they dead? Asleep? The darkness makes it hard to tell. A door opens. In the middle of a room, a dying fire in a hearth. Our arrival lights the oil lamps. Magical. Our nyctalopic escorts vanish as if dissolved by the light. Faces are illuminated. I instantly recognise four tousled braids. I have not seen Adjo since we left the caravanserai and boarded the *Diamant*. She is once again dressed in ordinary clothes, which is to say she is almost naked. In the room, there are a dozen women dressed just like her. We are the only three men. If, by any chance, a lustful thought should cross the wrong mind, the White Lady's stare brings us to our senses. Next to Adjo, the living statue of the afternoon sits enthroned on her gold stool. Madame Kaolin is Malan Alloua. I assume she is the queen, the wife of Akassimadou. In fact, she is the queen regent, Akassimadou's sister.

"Etiquette suggests I give you water first. But this afternoon you said your mouth was full of words and I would not wish you to swallow them."

Hardly have we sat down than she stares at me and speaks to me. At such times, royal protocol is abolished. Marks of deference are intended to be seen, and no eye can pierce the darkness or the walls. So, at night, people may speak more freely. I take the floor. Anno translates.

"The fluttering of the British flag is more and more deafening when the wind blows from the Gold Coast. And we should not entrust to the wind a friendship as old as that between our two peoples. The body of Amon-Ndouffou is still warm, his soul is still fresh, and it would be surly to forget that it was with us, the French, that he built the Krinjabo which now lies beneath our feet. Indeed, it is said that court councillors serve food given to them by France on British porcelain."

Amon-Ndouffou, the late king, friend of Verdier and Treich, was Akassimadou's uncle. It was he who signed the treaty linking the kingdom of Krinjabo to Louis-Phillipe's kingdom of France. Among the Anyi people, transfer of power is matrilineal and avuncular. It is inherited from one's maternal uncle, your mother's brother from the womb. Hence, an Anyi king has two possible kinds of successor: his sister's sons and his mother's brothers. All are legitimate. No rank is assigned by birth or generation. Among the Anyi, the legitimacy, acquisition, exercise and transmission of power is through the female line.

"No noble here speaks in the name of the Sanwi. The king is Akassimadou!"

By which she means: "I am king!" Malan Alloua's talents as a leader are so considerable that Amon-Ndouffou made no secret of the fact that, had she been a man, his niece would have inherited his crown. Akassimadou, Alloua's brother, suffered from polio as a boy, and, ever since, has depended on his sister to stay on his feet. She it was who carried him to the throne. In the kingdom of Krinjabo, to Akassimadou the tiara, to Malan the staff. I return to the word 'albino'.

"Nanan Verdier swore in the name of the Republic, the greatest fetish in all of France, that he would send Treich to Kong."

"If the spirits wish it, he will arrive there safely. The spirits accompany pure souls."

"Just as two hands wash each other, so Nanan Verdier made Nanan Amon-Ndouffou and Nanan Amon-Ndouffou made Nanan Verdier."

"Your word is true."

"It is in the natural order of things that a son should fulfil the work of his father."

"It is dark, Parisian! You can point to the cleft in my groin and no-one will take offence. Speak."

"The pact of Ahounyanssou."

In Africa, astonishment is never feigned. "Han!" the women gasp in unison. Bodies straighten, heads shake, Treich is calm, Anno turns to me. He has not time to translate. Alloua has understood. So too the others. A single word suffices: "Ahounyanssou".

* * *

There is something of a Catherine de Medici about Malan Alloua. Both are unprepossessing, both know how to wield a phial of poison. Many of their palace adversaries have supped death from their plates. Both are bigots whose intransigent religious convictions incline them to settle differences on sacred matters by bloody means. The French queen had heretics slaughtered by the thousand; the blood shed during the Saint Bartholomew's Day massacre is carved upon her heart. The African queen mother is an adept of fetishistic rituals that require accessories cut from the human anatomy. She has no taboos about how blood is collected, whether from the living or the dead.

Alloua, like Catherine, has a "flying squad". Krinjabo boasts the most beautiful women of the Anyi race, and since they are twice as numerous as their menfolk, even the most churlish man enters into marriage without cavil. A platoon of female courtesans hovers around the king's sister, who well knows how to dispatch them to defend her personal interests and those of the kingdom, even in the darkest enclaves of her most devious noblemen, or beneath the mosquito nets of the influential white men. Her baleful beauty spreads along the coast, as far as the British colonies. Alloua has no children of her own, no-one who might take the throne, but the king's other sisters and his aunts vie with each other to be in her good graces. They know that it is she who will choose the heir from among their sons. A mistress of coitus interruptus, she chooses and dismisses her lovers according to her whims and interests. All those who, in an excess of passion, have forgotten themselves and spattered her with semen have later served as sacrifice to some ritual. If, by chance, a male seed should impregnate her womb, Malan Alloua deploys her arcane knowledge of plants that act as abortifacients. This, in sum, is the woman with whom I am discussing the pact of Ahounyanssou.

For endless minutes, Alloua says nothing. She is once again the living statue she was this afternoon. Allowing silence to linger is a powerful word. At the court of her uncle, she learned how power is attained and wielded. The plume of smoke from the dying fireplace seems to emanate from her. The half-light does little to soften her unprepossessing face and her basilisk stare. The shadows cast on the wall are spectral. There could be no better illustration of a witches' coven. With a voice from beyond the grave, Malan the Manticore breaks the silence.

"Catheriny . . ."

She must be a mind reader. How else could she intuit my wild imaginings comparing her to Catherine de Medici?

"Son of Catheriny . . ."

She is not a mind reader. She has remembered my mother's name. I mentioned it during my "raising of the flag". Africans are good at remembering names and faces. In oral cultures, the register of names is a map drawn by the collective memory, which is enhanced by the very act of remembering.

". . . I did not dispatch Adjo to find you. Of all the women present, she is the only one I have never sent anywhere."

Anno and Treich glance at each other. I think they are snickering and indignant that, through my fault, we are talking about some maid in a pagne. In truth, though I alone have spoken, my two friends know better than I where this is leading. Accustomed to the parleys of the Anyi, they know that they often shift abruptly from pillar to post only to return.

"One of your ancestors lived among us. A man of great worth. It is said that a Fraynch king who vied with the very sun itself sent him here to us. He counselled our king and fought in the wars that established our authority over the savage Agwas, the brave Bonos, the stubborn Akans and the perfidious Apollonians, our chiefest enemies. Being a faithful companion, when the king died, this man demanded to accompany him to Blô, the land of our ancestors. The multi-branched sabre fell upon his neck. It was in his name, in the name of the victories he won, in the name of his supreme sacrifice, that we signed the treaty of Nanan Louis-Filippay, at a time when your Republik did not yet exist. And it was in his name that Nanan Amon-Ndouffou helped Nanan Verdier resist the Engerlish, even when there was not a single Fraynch rifle remaining on this entire coast. This man was the Parisian! Here he begot children and they begot descendants, one of whom is present. It was the voice of her ancestors who guided her to Grand-Bassam and to you."

On the wall, a shadow moves, a head with four tousled plaits. That unnaturally oval face, those lips much thinner than those of a woman from Bassam, that long, thin nose, so incongruous on such a black face . . . In the semi-darkness of this room, Adjo's features appear to me in a new and different light. With her face daubed in white, she would be the spit-and-image of a Countess Arnoult-de-Laménardière or a Milady Pimpterton. But her body is a miracle of proportions that has no equal, Black or white.

"Son of Catheriny, you heard the people of Krinjabo call you 'Parisian'. A single mouth may lie. A hundred voices in chorus, never. You have been here only a short time, yet you know much more about us than the fever-afflicted in Assinie or the diarrhoeics in Grand-Bassam. Your journey with us has only just begun. It will be a long one. You will not make the journey alone, this Malan Alloua says to you."

She tosses something to the ground that, in the half-light, is impossible to identify. Adjo unfurls. Her short knotted pagne makes her movements easy, and her legs cast slender shadows on the wall. She recites something inaudible over the object before sitting down again.

"Adjo Blé will accompany you, but her journey will end at the River Tanoé. You will return! The Parisian always returns."

I remember Adjo Blé sitting on the sandbank at Assinie. *Blé* means "black". By what mystery can skin that is much darker than that of ordinary Anyi woman be descended from a white man? Moreover, I find this story of a white man willingly mounting the steps of a sacrificial altar to allow himself to be beheaded in the name of a Black king unconvincing. Alloua is a master-manipulator of symbols. Christianity has been toying with symbols for centuries. Malan Alloua knows this too. She holds out her hand. In it, a pyramidal object glitters, and in Krinjabo, all that glitters is gold.

"Marcellay . . ."

I first hear Treich's Christian name from the lips of an Anyi regent as hideous and as wily as the devil. We are done with the post; we now return to the pillar.

"You have told us that you seek your white brother. The fetishes are unanimous: do not return with him. If you should find this man, kill him. Then cut off all those things that protrude – hair, nose, nails, sex – and toss them into the first river that blocks your return. In this way, his impure soul will not haunt you. If you do not have the strength, then give him up! He will die as all white men die here in our country, in the delirium of fever and a pestilential pool of diarrhoea. If you should bring him back to the coast, this man will devour your soul and you will disappear, leaving no descendants. When you reach Kong, give this to the Mensah. He will remember the pact. He will grant your requests. The matter is settled."

The Legend of the First Landing

"Are you certain that such things as white women exist?"

"My grandfather swears that he saw one in the Gold Coast."

"What kind of man travels so far without his wives?"

"And yet, they behave like normal men with our women. My niece confirmed as much to me about the captain this morning."

Such conversations were a commonplace among the people of Assinie until the morning when Madame Keller disembarked. The shock: she was completely clothed from head to toe. To cover a woman in such a manner! Wild imaginings raced in diametrically opposing directions. Many looked away, convinced that only the hideously ugly would cover up their bodies in such a fashion. The swelling beneath their pagnes marked out the others, who imagined her as Mummy Water. Like many Assinian fishermen, they believed in the legend that recounts how, in the deepest depths of the ocean, there dwells a race of women with white skin, shimmering hair and azure eyes, a description that perfectly fit Madame Keller. Mummy Water or monstrous gorgon? People were agreed on only one point: Monsieur Keller. The people deemed him full of good sense and respect, and were grateful to him for ending *the interrogations. They even offered him young maidens to take as second wives so they might help his wife with the heavy work with which she would be tasked in the fields. The couple settled in Élima, where Monsieur Keller tended the first coffee plantation while his wife opened the first classroom, long, long before the arrival of the bearded men with their crosses and their long white bubus.*

Louis Anno
Interpreter
Assinie

AN URBAN CHAPTER

ASSIKASSO

Hygiene is the chief concern of every Anyi household. At break of day, the women armed with brooms of palm bristles trace the dirt floor in arabesques, hunting down the smallest scrap of debris. The ballet of morning baths is launched by the chief patriarch of the courtyard. As he finishes his toilet, before wrapping himself in the traditional British pagne, he daubs his body with shea butter. His black skin becomes glossy as ebony. I can understand how the expression "ebony trade" came to refer to human cargo by the slave traders. Their ablutions completed, the mouth is widened using a wooden accessory, a stem cut from a root. They pick at their ivories with an energy that would leave a Périgord parishioner toothless. This daily routine explains in part the dazzling brilliance of African tooth enamel.

Usually, before bathing, children and adults indulge in an activity that is common to all mankind, but here is practised according to a curious ritual. An unripe pear, which has been cored, dried and pierced from the tapered end, is filled with a liquid of plant extracts and crushed chillies. Mothers grab their

151

children, insert the pointed end of the device into their anus, and, by blowing into the external cavity, propel the potion into their bowels. As soon as they are freed, you should see the little ones run to the nearest thicket to relieve themselves. Without a whit of embarrassment, the adults also perform the same ritual, women on women, men on men, before relieving themselves in some more distant patch of undergrowth. The echo of their flatulence can be heard from far away. Whereas the slightest gastric trouble triggers dysenteric torrents in Europeans, the intestinal tract of the Anyi needs to be motiv-ated in this manner. The couples who mutually administer this variant of Molière's device are marked by a rare trust. A poison introduced in this manner would be viciously effective. Brothers of the pear unto death! I shall find some other way to express my trust.

The women begin cooking before the dawn. The sun has not yet risen above the treetops when the first meal is served. In polygamous households, each wife prepares a meal. It falls to the patriarch to apportion the food. He does so with the gravity of a justice of the peace, according to rules of fairness that he alone knows. People eat according to age and sex. There is a single shared platter, one by one the hands dip in, beginning with the eldest. It is here that patience is learned. There is no clearer sign of a poor upbringing than a child who dips their hand into the plate in defiance of this protocol.

The *foufou* – balls of pounded yam – must be rolled by hand, dipped into a sauce, and make the journey to the lips without a drop being spilled. Not to do so is an affront to the Gospel according to D'jon, chapter 6. The palate quickly becomes accustomed to the chilli heat, especially since each mouthful is accompanied by a gulp of palm wine. My meals are less frequently accompanied by the sight of adults and children waiting for my face to turn puce so they can laugh. But not all dishes are hot. The African chilli pepper is a wild plant. They cannot be found all year round. And, as with mushrooms, the places where they grow are kept secret by each man.

The end of the morning repast signals the beginning of the day's activities. The women are the first to set off, heading to the fields. They tend the cultivated fields or forage for wild plants. The men are required only for heavy work, tilling a clearing or creating high beds in which to grow yams. So they take their time. Otherwise, the men prefer to spend their time hunting, tending the palms that provide wine, or chatting in the shade of the baobabs, aptly named palaver trees.

The lively brood of children, completely naked, frolic through the courtyards, the streets and the scrubland. With their shrill cries, their incomprehensible games, and the breakneck races even in the blazing heat of noon, they end up covered in dust and mud. When it is time for evening ablutions, they are hunted down, flushed out of every cache and hiding place. The epiphytes that hang from the tall baobabs are crushed to create sponges. The mothers or the kangah – the "hut slaves" – smear the children with a black soap made from red palm oil and grey banana ash and scrub them until they are as clean as they can be. Next the procession of adults once again makes its way to the tub. Hot water is used both morning and evening. It regenerates the body and wards off colds and chills. Dejean was right: the two or three degrees the thermometer dips at night are enough to create a sensation of numbness. It is not unusual to see children and adults alike with their teeth chattering when the temperature falls to 30°C. Sensory relativity.

The second meal of the day is served according to the same rituals as the first. Then, the smallest children gather around the fire for tales told by the family storyteller. The teenagers take to the main square or to discreet places to play flirtatious games. The adults convene in the courtyard, the dim huts or the dark forest for meetings, palaver, conspiracies, mysticism. If there is a tom-tom, no-one sleeps until the notes of the last drummer fade beneath the stars.

At Assikasso, no-one exposes their skin at night. Forced to vie with countless other insects, and hunted by various natural predators, the mosquitoes in the jungle are few. A far cry from the clouds and swarms in Grand-Bassam and Assinie. In building towns and cities we have created an imbalance that greatly benefits mosquitoes: our activities help our fiercest enemies thrive.

I have been appointed an official host. His name is Boidy; I go everywhere with him. My understanding of the Anyi and their customs has dramatically improved. I am Boidy's white fetish: a guest who brings honour and prosperity to his house. For once, this has nothing to do with the colour of my skin. A wise man would have told him of my arrival. I occupy the hut of his late father. In one corner there is an effigy representing a male, as evinced by an outrageously proportioned phallus. With short legs tucked beneath an excessively long torso leaning forward, and short arms folded over the chest, the figure looks as though it is ready to leap at the throat of an assailant. In the flattened face, a thick-lipped mouth is half parted to reveal a menacing row of teeth fashioned from slivers of bronze. Perched on the head is a container that holds the bones, the skull fragments and phalanges of illustrious ancestors. A reliquary! "*Swear that you will take the reliquary. It houses the voices of our ancestors. The stones . . .*" The last words of Father. I left without respecting his wishes: I left my ancestors back in La Galerette. Now, here in Assikasso, I sleep with those of Boidy. Using such a piece of wood, a sculptor needs only rudimentary adzes and knives to express history, symbols and religion. The artist is anonymous, he does not sign a work whose creation the Anyi people believe is guided by spirits on behalf of the whole society. Such an effigy is brought out only on rare occasions. Swear on it and you must keep your word. Fail, and you will be tormented to the point of madness. The Anyi people have no need of instruments of torture to extract a confession. An effigy is sufficient. Nothing is more terrifying than a fetish! A chicken in the case of an affront, a pagne for adultery, a goat for theft, an ox for a land dispute, and, above all, a life for a life. Anyi justice is not about punishment but about recompense. In a case of murder, the clan of the guilty party may be ordered to give a child, a woman or a young man to the victim's family. The clan pays because guilt is collective. It is not uncommon to see a "recompense" cross the street to lead a peaceful life with his new family, ignoring the old one. The concept of prison does not exist, so the word has no Anyi equivalent. For those guilty of the most heinous crimes, the punishment is post-mortem. When they die, their bodies are mutilated and, rather than being interred, are thrown into an accursed wood. In this way, an evil soul can never find rest, and if, by some extraordinary chance, it is reincarnated, it can be recognised by its stigmata. Such an idea of justice implies a capacity for forgiveness that dwarfs that of the Christian. For the living, capital punishment entails expulsion from the clan, forced exile far from one's family, one's tribe, one's ancestors.

I record all my observations of the Anyi people of Assi-kasso in a notebook. A written report is the first duty of the colonialist. Treich even considers it his most important responsibility, and one he performs every evening. "You must understand, Dabilly, our lives here are so precarious that we should see our presence as part of a relay race. These note-books are our sole witness." The weeks that have passed since I left the caravanserai on the outskirts of Assikasso seem like months.

* * *

"In the jungle, news travels faster than the traveller," says Treich. On our way back to Assikasso, no-one in the villages was surprised to see us. In these uncharted lands, we were more than expected. Man is an animal that feeds on curiosity. The more distant a stranger, the warmer his welcome. He is feted even as a neighbour is ignored. In Yakassé, after a feast of giant snails and huge prawns, we abandoned an ecstatic Dreyfus to the contemplation of a field of holes averaging ten metres in depth. "When you dig as deep as this, you're not searching for something, you've found it..." In the kingdom of Bettié, Bénié Kwamin, whom we presumed hostile, gave us a most remarkable welcome before signing the treaty.

Article 1: The king of Bettié hereby declares that he has placed his country under the protectorate of France.

Article 2: Trade in the kingdom of Bettié shall be freely conducted only with the French. The king of Bettié will ensure that the routes in his domain are open to all French companies.

Two sentences and a scrawled X and the kingdom is ours. Eight articles read aloud before the chief and his court. The last, recited just before signing, established the indemnities and personal compensation to the chief... At Attakrou, the chief was so proud to have a visiting caravan of two white men that he immolated a regiment of goats. It was at this point, just before we crossed the Tanoé, that Adjo turned back. She had not addressed a word to me since Krinjabo, but her eyes spoke volumes. I let nothing of my heartbreak show... In Allangouanou, Chief Edoukou, sporting a braided beard some fifty centimetres long, demanded a white son among his descendants. "Better to have a piece of meat in all the village sauces. One can never know what tomorrow will bring." He offered Treich his daughter in marriage. A polite refusal. Edoukou turned to me, physically holding out the frightened girl's hand. A categorical refusal. Anno assured me that Adjo would not be offended, that I would not have to honour both at the same time, on the same bed; that the two would make an excellent household, being cousins. An outraged refusal. This prompted a laugh between Anno and the chief.

We often laugh at our own expense. During our explorations, we too are being explored. In the villages, every time

I go to heed the call of nature, I am followed by a horde of curious onlookers. No thicket is dense enough for privacy when children and adults alike want to know how we make stools, what colour they are and what they smell like. Many are disappointed ... At Amélékia, Kassi Dihiè did not receive us. He preferred to trade with the British who had subjugated Ashanti country. Even so, he warmly embraced Treich, whom he had accompanied on part of his previous expedition.

"You are my friend, my hut is your hut, but what I see looming concerns more than just us two. It concerns our peoples. The Ashanti, our suzerain, have been defeated by the Inglissys. We can serve no-one but our masters' masters. You may stay here as many nights as you need to persuade me otherwise."

Though Kassi Dihiè did not sign an X to a piece of parchment, he organised a feast as memorable as that in Attakrou ... Everywhere, Treich's personality ensured that our journey would be auspicious. Nature herself smiled on us, and the rains were rare. Once, as we were fording a river, a crocodile seized the arm of a porter. The others tried to beat it off with sticks. One even pulled it by the tail. Eventually the reptile released its grip when fired on by a rifleman, Coumba. Despite his mangled limb, the victim was mocked by his colleagues, who mimicked his thrashing in the water. This naive theatricality, this unbridled laughter, was contagious. Having escaped the reptile's maw, the survivor finally had his revenge on those who mocked him after I daubed him with tincture of iodine and wound pristine bandages over the deepest bites. This was the only hitch we encountered before we reached Assikasso.

* * *

Assikasso. Latitude 7°5'12" according to Dejean; land of gold according to Dreyfus; rubber capital according to Fourcade; gateway to Bondoukou according to Treich. My trading post. There is no vanity in that possessive. Scarcely a hint of pride. When called upon to build alone, in adversity, far from everything, you *make* things your own. My outpost, my boy, my interpreter, my Senegalese infantrymen, my porters, my land... The colonial spirit is founded on ownership. Never get carried away. Do as Treich does: deliberately downplay the official actions of which we are mere pawns on the board of history. The basis for our outpost in Assikasso is the fruit of a treatise signed with the chiefs of the Indenie kingdom during Treich's previous expedition. We agreed to build on the outskirts of the village, atop a hill near the trail used by the caravans of pedlars from Bondoukou. Building on a hilltop affords more than mere strategic and symbolic advantages; the relative altitude protects us from the pernicious miasma. Winds prevail over infection. Wherever the topography permits, we build our outposts on high ground.

* * *

This matter settled, Treich's caravan moved on. The transfer of the flag took place to a salvo of four shots fired by fifteen Chassepots, giving our farewells a solemnity of great effect. I stayed behind with Coumba, Soumaré and Sall, three Senegalese infantrymen; Sokhna, Amar, Camara and Kady, wives of the aforementioned infantrymen; Mamadou and Petit Malamine, their bawling offspring who were permanently secured, one to Sokhna's rump, the other to Amar's, or perhaps the other way round; Angaman-Kouadio, known as Captain Lucky, an interpreter; and Kassy Ntiman, a boy cook of about fifteen, who is furious that I have not given him a French name.

Yafoun, from his camp at Yafounkro, and Éhiwa, from his camp on the outskirts of Anyi-Bilékro, are the kings of Assikasso. Not that they vie with each other for power, but both rule. Yafoun's strength and brutality are feared by all, including his alter ego. Éhiwa's wisdom and intelligence are respected by all, including his alter ego. Any cause from the lips of only one of them is doomed in advance. Éhiwa is too afraid of Yafoun's wrath, Yafoun of some ruse by Éhiwa. Only the most skilled rhetorical acrobats know how to vault over Yafoun's frontal attacks without falling into Éhiwa's sibylline machinations. The palaver drags on so long it would try the patience of a saint. The town's four thousand inhabitants live in the image of the governing dichotomy. A community from Apollonia on the Gold Coast exerts a British influence over the part of the populace embodied by Yafoun. The other part leans towards the French Tricolour that flutters above the Éhiwa hut. The town is also home to a group of Mandé-Dyulas who moved here from Djimini, Damalla, Kong and Bondoukou, as much to ply their trade as street hawkers as to flee the territorial expansion of a Black conqueror named Samory. There is even a courtyard of Krumen huts, far removed from the first waves of the Atlantic. Thus comprised of peoples from very different horizons, Assikasso is not merely a collection of Anyi people. It is a real town, the first one I have encountered, whose urban life is not of our creation. I walk around in city shoes, the Gospel according to Saint Dejean. Shoes are the accessory that attracts most curiosity. The locals even genuflect to verify that they are not a singular extension of our anatomy.

It takes some three weeks to build the French concession. A hut with a dual function as an administrative office and my personal accommodation; a second hut, styled as a mess hall, houses the Senegalese infantrymen and their families; a third, our Ministry of Trade, is built to house passing caravans. The three huts form an isosceles triangle with sides measuring forty paces. At the centre, a flagpole from which our flag will fly. To everyone's astonishment, I take an active role in the work. The White Man does not work, especially in the sun. He makes others work. Flushing after even the slightest exertion, I am the laughing stock of the Anyi and Mandé-Dyula labourers. The former, being animists, are paid in crates of gin; the latter, being Mohammedans, in textiles and tobacco. While I wait for my Versailles to be completed, my temporary accommodation becomes something of an affair of state. Each kingdom wants me to reside with them, and many notables vie to welcome me. It requires a whole night of palaver in the presence of the kings to resolve the issue. Boidy Akou, a notable from Yafoun, prevails, since his courtyard is equidistant from Yafounkro, the Yafoun district, and Anyi-Bilékro, the Éhiwa camp. His compound boasts seven huts in a semicircle around a communal courtyard. These he shares with three wives, a squadron of children, a phalanx of nephews and nieces, a platoon of "hut captives" (kangah), four sheep, seven nanny goats, a noisome billy goat that utters a raucous rutting call, and a host of chickens, to which is now added one white man.

* * *

When my Versailles is completed, I cannot leave "my parents" without a celebration worthy of my rank. Boidy also wants to mark the departure of his "white fetish". Since the quality of the reception reflects the prestige of its host, he sacrifices half his flock of goats. The billy goat will now have only three females to satisfy his piercing libido. A goodly number of hens and cockerels complete the carnage. The neighbourhood provides jars of palm wine. I contribute a roll of percale and two cases of Royal Stork Gin. The dark green bottles, wider at the neck than at the base, are curious parallelepipeds. The label claims that the two litres of 40° proof alcohol are produced in Delftshaven near Rotterdam. On one side, a drawing of six silver coins – in fact it depicts the obverse and reverse of three medals – proclaims that the beverage has swayed the palates of three international juries: Gold Medal London, Exposition Universelle Paris, Nederlandse Industrie Tentoonstelling. Den-Den, "Medals", is the local nickname for this gin. Ancestors, djinns, sorcerers, fetishes and every Anyi old enough to stand on two legs concur with these eminent juries. The gift of a single bottle customarily provokes dancing and merriment. What then of two whole cases? Their appearance provokes the loudest cheer ever heard below the Tropic of Cancer. The tom-tom strikes up.

In the circle, the dancers, male and female, launch into a series of pyrrhic dances. The repetitive rhythm is mesmeric.

Nothing akin to the four-four time of French popular songs or the three-four time of waltzes. At first, the drummers' passion sounds like unbridled chaos. Listen more intently and you can hear the four beats slipping under the three, meeting on each twelfth beat to form a loop. Bach employs this stratagem in short passages; the Anyi do so all night long. A lone voice launches into a solo to which the assembled company responds in chorus: the structure of the songs is crude, but hugely enriched by the participation of the whole circle. Harmonies abound. From everywhere, solos soar without ever vying with each other. For the Anyi, waiting one's turn is something learned the moment they leave their mother's womb, at their first communal meal. Furtively, I count the beats. I am alone in doing so, but it lets me know when the chorus will arrive. The drums regularly change hands without any loss of dexterity. "Art" does not exist in the Anyi vocabulary. Each is creator and observer, actor and audience. An entire orchestra. With the singing and the Den-Den, the night grows feverish.

An intoxicating beauty drags me from my seat. I respond to her vigorous invitation as best I can. While I do not know what my legs are doing, my head is thinking of Adjo. In such a circle, she could use her grace to its fullest. My inhibitions fade into the darkness, washed down by gin, by pounding rhythms and palm wine. Before my eyes, my partner's breasts move in harmonic phases, their effect like that of the hypnotist's pendulum. She advances and retreats, twirls and pirouettes. During one such arabesque, her pagne flies off, she catches it in mid-air, and flourishes it with a hand that has no immediate intention of replacing it. The crowd erupts. The dancer is not completely naked: her Queen Victoria kerchief protects the ultimate triangle of her modesty. With her fluttering loincloth, she dabs the sweat from my face before re-tying it about her waist, never missing a beat. The crowd is at fever pitch. Boidy now enters the circle. Three small steps forward, two back, body bowed, neck tensed, arms outspread as though steadying himself against a fall, Boidy gracefully advances, in synchronised rhythm with my convulsive entrechats, my chaotic tremor. His "white fetish" is dancing. Through his generosity, his nobility, his importance, he, Boidy, has caused the white man to dance himself into a trance before the hut of his ancestors. He lifts up my arm. The cheers grow wilder. The circle becomes a pandemonium.

The collective frenzy has not abated when I hear a cock crow. But a cock that crows: "Have you seen Bismarck?" in a cry that can down out such a din is nowhere recorded, not even in a bestiary that pre-dates Genesis. What devilry is this! Back in Châteauneuf, on nights when the Alsatians celebrated new manacles, someone would always say, "Have you seen Bismarck?" Each man in turn had to improvise a response. The last line of each verse was: "Bismarck has been fucked" with something "up his arse". In Assikasso, no-one has reason to bear a grudge against the Iron Chancellor, least of all the cockerels. Where then does that tune come from? Suddenly, the tom-toms, singers, dancers, talkers and drinkers stop. All have heard this incongruity. In the ensuing silence, I am able to identify the instrument. The circle parts and Soumaré enters, a flagpole and tumescent Tricolour rising from his groin. Behind him, Coumba, his cheeks puffed out, lips pressed to the mouthpiece of a bugle. Next to him is Sall, followed by twelve infantrymen freshly recruited from Djimini. They march in step, Chassepots slung over their shoulders. In a reflex I thought alien to me, I snap to attention and perform a military salute that is surely questionable. The troop halts in front of me before turning back. The Republic is calling; it is time for me to return to my hilltop. I fall into line with the procession, marching in a goose-step, drunk on music and alcohol. Cheers from the Anyi. In the infantry, "Have you seen Bismarck?" is the tune used to sound the retreat.

* * *

On Tuesday and Thursday, the market days in Assikasso, I march between the stalls with my two infantrymen and my flag-bearer. An idea dreamed up by Coumba to impress the Apollonian traders, mollifying their hostility while drawing attention to the various French goods. The crowds jostle and part to allow us to pass, only to immediately close up as though we had not suddenly burst into the market. Trading resumes, there is no stopping it. Commerce is the key to this historic movement.

Visiting the market, I become aware that not a single Englishman is pulling strings to undermine our influence. Indeed, our saleable exports have long since become sovereign. Via the hands of the suppliers, it is our exports that determine colonial conquest and the battle between the European powers. Exports are the initial colonists. For centuries now, without our help, far pre-dating our most intrepid explorers, our exports have penetrated the lands, the people and the minds of Africa. Reappropriated and reinterpreted to the point that they seem sometimes to be the emanation of African genius, many have become traditional objects. A king is naked without his fringed parasol; spirits are mute without gin; needles and nails augment the power of fetishes; elegance without the use of talcum powder is unseemly; a coquette without a pagne is poor; a rich man without a bowler hat is destitute; a dowry without salt is heresy; even if resulting in hundreds of deaths, a war without guns is just a skirmish; and what can be said of gunpowder, which has been redrawing borders for centuries? Goods are efficient colonists. No dysentery or bilious fever troubles a skein of yarn; no madness threatens a bar of soap or a demijohn of brandy; there are no casualties, no bloody ambushes in the battle of rum versus wine . . . Goods are enduring colonists. We are here only as a physical presence and to collect scrawled Xs on paper.

Our first trades took place on the beach. Items of novelty, variety, curiosity, gimcrack, a profusion of shapes and colours . . . Amid the muted green of the vegetation, the dull grey of the skies, the gloom of the topography, such items are immediately appealing. In exchange, the Africans offer the things that nature provides in abundance, those that are easily harvested and transported. Worthless things that we call "products". Ivory, for example, is simply collected from elephant graveyards. When a pachyderm is slaughtered, the meat is eaten, the tail is made into fly whisks, the hair is plaited into bracelets so strong that they are handed down from generation to generation, but the tusks . . . By exchanging elephant tusks for glassware and coloured fabrics, the Apollonian boatman thinks the Dutch sailor a fool and he in turn believes that he is dealing with a cretin. An exchange in which both parties are dupes. Value may be relative, but the lure of profit is universal. Over time, the list of goods and products grows longer. A mutual escalation. Even "ebony" is traded! After a time, value is no longer relative. One side of the scale prevails, the side that delivers and takes away. Ever since Father's beloved Romans or Attila's Huns, the civilisation on the move is the one that prevails. Today, the British and the French are pushing products further and further inland. They are delivering the goods themselves. The chain of intermediaries will wither away. The balance of values will tip even more in our favour. It is inevitable.

"We calmly signed the paper of Treissy the white. Wisdom and temperance are great counsellors. But if Wossily, the mad British raider, asks, we shall sign his too. Force and terror are great counsellors. Your piece of paper is meaningless. What matters is our sword word, and that we shall give to whoever makes us the best offer. In the meantime, Franssay or Inglissy, settle your differences before you come to visit. You may fly your flag on any hill you choose, but not in the village square."

Boidy concludes the palaver prompted by my request to the council. Needless to say, it takes a whole night to come to a decision. Boidy is both a spy for my quests and an ambassador for my requests. The Anyi of Assikasso were clever to billet a crucial guest like me in the home of a wily notable like Boidy. But their view of the colonial situation is outdated. For us, all that matters is the parchment; the spoken word has no currency. A simple rule prevents any war between European powers. Since Berlin, Treaty + Effective Presence = Colony. The X on Treich's treaty, together with my presence, seals the fate of their kingdom. With or without my flag fluttering in the village square, they are now French. Though Bondoukou is not yet, alas, which is our chief concern.

Playing on the hesitation between the French and the British, the council divides and conquers. The Apollonians will already have rushed to tell the British post in Koomassee: "Frenchman in Assikasso. Another to reach Bondoukou!" The British counter-attack is inevitably on its way. But whether we or they prevail, only one civilisation will triumph. No-one at the Yafoun–Éhiwa council has realised this yet. Not even Boidy.

A CHAPTER ON WASPS AND BEES

ASSIKASSO EPP 1 AND EPP 2

In the big schoolyard, beneath the whole wide sky, EPP Assikasso 2 stands right opposite EPP Assikasso 1, a building with six classrooms. The national flag sprouting from the mast marks an invisible border between the two. At break time, for some reason I don't yet understand, crossing this border provokes the wrath of the raised heads opposite. Apparently, the two schools are enemies. I have trouble recognising the friendly faces; how am I supposed to recognise the others? All the boys are black with frizzy hair and Belgian shorts and shirts. The girls don't make any more effort, with their identical hair in braids from their foreheads to their necks. Maman sometimes has braids like that, I like them, but she never wants to braid my hair. She tells me she can't on account of the rust that took the frizz out of my hair when I was born. I understand that hair stuff is for girls. In the schoolyard the trees and the sky are filled with loads of birds. Not like back in the Oude Kerk where there's just the pigeons, who go to church more often than the people, but lots of different types, colours, sizes, songs. The big ones fly so high they look like someone's drawn them on the sky. The little ones fly so low you think you could catch them. A yellow-black squadron flies past at ground level. I'm so busy following them with my feet and my eyes that I don't see the leg stuck out to trip me. When I get up from the bitten dust, there's a boy standing right in front of me. From what my eyes can judge, he's a head taller than Moody Marko. He's got a broken front tooth in his mouth that flashes as he laughs at me. He's being a bully. He doesn't know he's dealing with a champion of class warfare.

"What's the little Dutch baby doing away from Maman's apron strings?"

Why does everyone have it in for Maman, who's a fucking socialist and doesn't sell kisses and never wears skirts? A Moody Marko with a head full of stiff braids. Hair-pulling isn't going to work. I grab his ear so fast and so hard that I think it's come off in my hand. All the other kids did too. But ears stick to the head even more than hair does. Headmasters, school-masters, schoolmistresses and everyone in the schoolyard under the whole wide sky hear the boy's ear-y cry. As usual, I find myself sprawled on the ground. Trying to pull us apart makes the boy scream louder. Geneviève shouts, "Anouman!", the name Maman gave me. It's the first time I've heard it since Maman went to Comrade Hodja's Albananianist paradise. I let go of the kid's ear and she lets go of mine. In this hellish African alien nation colony, lying in the dust, with a huge boy dancing a jig over me, I realise the class struggle is international. Marx and his Angles were right. "Workers of all countries, unite!"

Second house arrest under the photo of *His Excellency The President of the Republic*. Light suit, dark tie, he looks like a foreman who has sold himself out to the bosses; the medi-evil bourgeois throwback looks older in the photo hanging over the headmaster's desk. He looks like a Versifailleur. Comrade Papa would have hanged him alive at dawn. Geneviève and the headmaster are in the middle of another debate about education and culture, the culture of education, education in culture, culture in education . . . When they talk like that, I don't understand a word of their French, but I know how to classify it in Comrade Papa's filing cabinet. The headmaster talks in the past tense, he misses the time when there were no televisions in classrooms. Geneviève talks in the future tense, hoping for a time when there'll be televisions in every classroom. The headmaster is backward-looking. Geneviève is forward-thinking. The debate comes round to me.

"It's my fault, I should have talked to him, told him that here children never fight at school."

"Geneviève, everyone here has culture shock. At the start of every school year, dozens of children show up from refugee camps with three words of French in their back pocket and only the vaguest idea of what they'll find."

"Amsterdam is a lot further away, and you couldn't call it a refugee camp . . ."

"But like the kids who come to us from the camps, he comes from a culture and a language that are completely different from French. If all the kids started fighting because they had culture shock, the schoolyard would be like Katanga . . ."

"Did you say Katanga, Comrade Headmaster? That's in the East Congo, it's the region of Africa that's sold its soul to big business, it's full of CIAs and killer spies and fermenters of military coups. They were the ones behind the international plot that murdered Lumumba the travelling beer salesman and stopped King Leopold's Congo being independent."

Geneviève, the headmaster and His Excellency The President of the Republic are all silent for a few minutes. I'm always annoying people, but they're more annoyed than usual.

"Where was I? Oh yes, it's definitely not cultural. The problem is the way he's been raised. Everyone knows his father, a rabble-rouser whose name has been mentioned in at least one attempted coup. We need to detoxify this child or we'll have serious trouble. Un-ques-tion-ably."

* * *

The She-Devil has a tail attached to a kiss-seller's outfit made from a black cow's hide. When I'm going home from school, having to walk past her window is like a Communist Party membership card: obligatory. I show my teeth, she sticks out her tongue. We've been doing it since I had baby teeth and she had a whore's tongue. After the She-Devil, just before the Mary Poppins and all the Scheherazades, is the window of windows. Having televisions in a shop window is counter-revolutionary on account of televisions are the shop windows of blind stateless big capitalism. It's the smoking gun of capitalism. It buys up workers' consciences by advertising the stuff they make in the factory. The worker is doubly exploited: when he makes things in the factory and when he buys those things. Comrade Papa is even tougher about television than he is about religious people's opium. It has to be wrested from the hands of the bourgeoisie and transformed into a tool for popular education.

Until that day comes, I'm outlawed from watching television. In the shop window, almost every set has Philips on it. Those bourgeois collaborators don't just sell fixed lights for ceilings, they also sell moving lights in boxes. I always pass the window at the same time because school always finishes at the same time and I always take the same way home. It's like with the women who sell kisses, you look in the window and go inside to choose. On the screens, a woman cut in half is talking, but you can't hear her because she's turned down. The woman inside the box is saying things about people from all over the world. The names of countries where there's disasters or wars scroll across a strip that covers her gentlemen's all-sorts. South Africa, Israel, Nicaragua, Lebanon and Palestine must love it. I'm going to get a public hanging if Comrade Papa catches me standing in front of the window of windows where I'm outlawed. Luckily, apart from the She-Devil and the flickering screens, there's no-one to see me betraying the class struggle.

MALA UNI

LUNA

TiPO

At EPP Assikasso 2, I'm completely inlawed to watch the television. All the sets are marked Thomson. I don't know them.

Thomson is teaching me loads of new stuff. A Mala is a three-fingered hand. A Tipo is like a Mala with pointy bits. A Luna is shaped like a haricot bean. These new shapes come in all sorts of different types: plain, striped, with dots, with holes. Plain Mala, polka-dot Luna, polka-dot Tipo with holes ... Awata-the-sorcerer is a man with a mane of hair so big that it can hide all the secrets of the universe created by the fat fart that made the Big Bang. We know the laws of motion, but we're still looking for the name of the guy who farted the stars ... Séa takes us on wonderful journeys so that we can discover the whole world without leaving our school desks ... Maloko is so fast asleep that a snake can swallow him whole and explain how food is digested in a long tube ... Yao is toto-logical, like a kid. His mistakes help us learn the complements of objects and the adjectives of all qualifiers. Yao makes the class laugh every time he climbs a pineapple tree ... Mikip is the opposite of Yao. He can dance, act, draw farted stars and master pieces and lots of other things that make everyone's eyes wide, even the teacher's ... Joe-the-little-boom-boom is a boy who got stung by a magic bee. Now he's so tiny he can ride on the back of a bee like it's the Flying Dutchman, and he has amazing adventures in the beehive and the fields all around. The bees built him a hexagonal house with walls made of wax and taps that pour honey. The queen bee is madly in love with Joe. But in order to populate the hive, she does sex with drones and has lots of bee-babies. The war against the wasps rallies up the working classes. Joe is a heroic general in the bee armies. His alliance with the genuine bumblebees puts the wasps on sting-sting routes. There's a final battle between Joe and Taurus, the wasp leader. The queen bee is even more in love with Joe after he wins, but she can't stop doing sex and having bee-babies ... Malas, Tipos, Lunas, Awata, Séa, Maloko, Yao, Mikip, Joe and many others are on the working-class television. There's no washing powders, no fizzy drinks, no disasters and no wars covering a woman's gentlemen's all-sorts. In every classroom across the country, every day, at the same time, it's the same proletarian programme for everyone. Comrade Papa would be happy. Here, even television is revolutionary.

Every morning starts with the bawling. Last name, first name. The teacher bawls out the list of high-heads. Those that are present stand up and shout: "Present!" When the present is absent, the response is even louder. As one man, the whole class shouts: "Absent!" The pupils laugh a lot at my first names during the bawling. I don't understand what some Alexander in a medi-evil world has to laugh about Shaoshan, which is the Great Helmsman's middle name. A Pierre or a Jacques from Palestine back when they were making the opium of the people is rubbish compared to an Illitch or a Davidovitch from the glorious Red October. I'm very proud during bawling because the teacher pronounces all the first names Comrade Papa gave me exactly right. At De Wallen, they never used those names. Probably because of the trembling at a communistic revolution. We're slap-bang in the middle of Patient Zero. Over there, I'm just Anouman, the bird man, the name that Maman gave me.

After the bawling comes the big reveal. The starter button for the Thomson is kept in a little cage. Before he reaches into his pocket for the key to the desk drawer where the key for the television is kept, the teacher slowly rotates his wrist, pushes up the sleeve of his multicoloured Dutch wax-print shirt, and checks his watch. He only does it for form's sake because anyone with a brain, like Awata-the-sorcerer, knows the teacher's next sentence will start: "It is 8.17 a.m., we now go to the

177

televisual teaching assistant. Today . . ." Thomson is turned on under fire from hundreds of pairs of eyes. Proletarian television is amazing. I never fall asleep, even when I stay up all night busy writing in Émile and Geneviève's books. In fact, no-one falls asleep in proletarian television classes. On the contrary. All heads are held high until Mikip says:

"Oh my! I've lost track of time. It's playtime . . ."

And the whole working-class class joins in as one man: "See you later, children!"

Making an enemy scream under the whole wide school-yard sky makes you the hero of EPP Assikasso. Even better, it makes me a hero to Yafoun Aléki, who sits next to me in proletarian television class. "You're very brave." In her notebook she writes this sentence from Yolanda's mouth in the same curvy letters Maman uses in her Kim Il Sung book. I come down with a teary eye. One of the advantages of sitting in the front row is she's the only one who sees it, the advantage of sitting up front. At Mikip's playtime, I don't have the invisible boundary of the step with the flag sprouting from it. I'm free to run wherever I like. And so do the other raised heads. The spoils of my international class war with Éhiwa Jean, the boy with the ear.

"No more fighting and, above all, absolutely no more revolutionary speeches," the headmaster insists when I'm in his office with Geneviève. His lips make a big round "O" when I tell him that this is unacceptable unless I get something in return. In education, headmasters are the bosses and pupils are the workers. And workers should never just accept the boss's diktat. We have to have collective union bargaining. I sit down.

"In the good old days, no pupil would dare raise his voice to teachers, let alone the headmaster. These children need discipline! We're not a centre for educational excellence anymore, we're just window dressing, reduced to listening to inane voices shouting 'Bravo!' when anyone gives an answer that's vaguely accurate. And then there's this terrible cartoon about a 'pineapple tree' that we can't correct until next year . . . Everyone in the world knows that a pineapple is not a tree, it's a bromeliad – everyone except the great and the good who produce children's education programmes. To the children, we're a laughing stock. We have to stop this thing in its tracks before it's too late. Even symbolically, we're humiliated. Time was, the teacher's desk was on a raised platform, he dominated the whole class. Now there's a television hanging over his head. It makes pupils insolent, impertinent and aggressive."

"But this boy didn't grow up with televisions in school. What are you talking about?"

"He's white! Like all the TV engineers and technicians. And they fill these bloody goggle boxes with white education. Add to that what we know about his father . . ."

Geneviève says nothing to the headmaster. She simply looks at me. There is a smile in her eyes when she sees me cross my legs and propose a motion. "Point of order, Comrade Headmaster . . ." I don't remember how long the negotiations lasted, but I won a big victory.

I'm allowed to run across all the invisible borders beneath the whole wide schoolyard sky and I'm allowed to call the adults "comrade sir". In return, I swear on the head of Comrade

Mao that I will never start a fight or make a single reference to the revolution under the wide schoolyard sky.

Yafoun Aléki follows me around everywhere. She talks a lot to me, but I don't answer much because my French is only good for talking revolution and I don't want to violate my union settlement with Comrade-Monsieur-Headmaster. Whenever we bump into Éhiwa Jean and his cabal, Yafoun Aléki claps her hands over her two ears and hides her laughing teeth. That's all. There's no legs stuck out to trip me. Éhiwa Jean and his cabal head off to the mango trees. Yafoun Aléki says it's a schoolyard revolution. I think she's playing devil's avocado, tempting my fate. I carry on right to the front of EPP Assikasso 1, under the coconut tree where my favourite yellow-black birds live. They've turned the coconut tree into a construction site for the masses. Birds don't have bosses, or leaders, they're all workers. Strand by strand, they strip away the leaves and use them to build nests, all the same shape and size, in the branches. When you're in the schoolyard, you don't need to talk about the revolution, you just look up into the trees.

"Thank you."

"What for?"

"This is the first time I've ever been here during playtime."

"Why?"

"Because people always keep to their own side."

"What people?"

"All the schools keep to their own territory."

"What territory?"

"Hey! You've only just got here and already you're like Mikip with all your questions."

"What do you mean?"

"Forget about it . . . Gangs, territories, it's like everything that's happened since episode one of Joe-the-little-boom-boom."

You can never talk quietly under a tree full of yellow-blacks. Birds like that are always screaming at each other on account of their classless society. And there's hundreds of them in the coconut tree. So Yafoun Aléki explains loudly. EPP Assikasso 1 are the wasps and Jean Éhiwa is like Taurus, their leader. Assikasso 2 is the beehive. Assikasso 1 territory includes the coconut trees. Assikasso 2 gets the mango trees. There are coconuts all year round, but there's only mangoes for three months of the year. In the class war between the bees and wasps, mango season, the season of the sweetest fruit, is the toughest. Yafoun Aléki tells me about the great battles fought. She doesn't mention a leader of the bees. I work that one out for myself. For the first time since she started talking, I bow my head. The coconut casts shadows of its branches and the little houses of the yellow-blacks over the blue-and-white checks of her dress. Yafoun Aléki is beautiful. But she's already Joe-the-little-boom-boom. And I can't really see myself being the queen bee.

The Legend of Sergeant
Malamine Camara

Citizens of Brazzaville. In this rich and ancient Venetian family, it was not rare for a boy to lose himself in an atlas and dream of new horizons. After all, their family tree included prestigious branches: a Caesar, emperor of Rome, and two doges, regents of the Crowned Republic of Venice and Genoa. Bringing civilisation to foreign climes was second nature to them. But Pietro's parents could not fathom the boy's passion for France, its language, its history, its culture, even its regional traditions. As an adolescent, he demanded to be allowed to pursue his studies at a lycée in Paris. His parents consented and, using their many contacts, ensured that he attended the very best. The Italian notion of family. After studying at this elite establishment, he enlisted in the French navy. When war broke out, Pietro, like all the citizens of France, wished to wage war against the Kaiser. However, people mistrusted all those who did not sport the correct colours on the three stripes of their flag. An "Italian" with an accent one could cut with a bayonet was suspect. While he languished in a barracks in Brittany, far from the battle-fields of the Ardennes and a historic defeat, Pietro did not forsake his love of France. He naturalised and became Pierre. He trained as a junior naval officer by accepting postings aboard ships on which no-one wished to serve. While sailing along the equatorial coast of Africa, he espied a wide estuary that planted in him the idea of a northern tributary which might join the Congo upstream, far from the raging torrents that flowed into the ocean. The hour of Pierre the explorer was at hand. Such an expedition was hardly a priority in a France financially crippled by reparations after its misadventure in the Ardennes. So Pierre turned to his family. All dipped their hands into their very deep pockets. What matter if it were in the name of a foreign nation? The Italian notion of family. Pierre engaged a team of porters, boatmen and guides, guarded by a dozen Senegalese infantrymen, among them Sergeant Malamine.

Pierre and Malamine immediately got along famously. The neo-Frenchman admired the physical vivacity and the intelligence of the neo-colonial subject. The neo-colonial subject loved the neophyte colonist who looked him in the eye, had a sing-song accent and spoke French with none of the "hoor'sun" "clod'pate", "haf'wit" and "f'koff" of the tattooed thugs of the Disciplinary Company in Dakar and Saint-Louis. Malamine could scarce believe his discourses on the equality between all the peoples on earth, even between Black and white. But he loved the gentleness in the man and the passion in his voice. Throughout the long voyage, Pierre treated all peoples with respect. There was still slave trading in the region. Decades after "abolition", the Portuguese continued their traffic in "ebony" along the coast. Every time they encountered such a caravan, Pierre paid a handsome sum to secure the freedom of dozens of slaves. Malamine would whisper the protocol in his ear. The conveyors, paid by night far from prying eyes, would vanish into the jungle, only too happy not to have to trek as far as the coast to make a profit from their "cargo". At dawn, the slaves were gathered around a flagpole where they would kneel and kiss the Tricolour, then Pierre would solemnly pronounce them freemen.

Pierre's stomach seemed to serve merely as an organ of temporary transit. Everything he ate or drank was immediately expelled, undigested, in the nearest available thicket. Malamine had seen white men suffer from diarrhoea, but Pierre's enteropathy surpassed all others'. Faced with his frequent absences and his increasing frailty, Malamine took the lead in all the planning. When, finally, they reached the banks of the Congo, they were no longer the eager exploration party that had set out. As the "gifts" dried up, many of the guides had deserted the caravan. All that remained were a handful of porters and three infantrymen, including Malamine. The Bateke-Tyo people, masters of the right bank of the river, greeted them with great enthusiasm, happy that the "good white man" was first to arrive. They had heard that a "bad white man", dubbed M'bula Matari (breaker of rocks), was also approaching. Henry Morton Stanley, a Welshman and naturalised American citizen, was forging a path using sticks of dynamite in the name of the king of Belgium. When he encountered natural obstacles, he did not go around them, he blew them up.

During their meeting with the Makoko Ilho, the spiritual leader of the region, Malamine added two huge wild boar, four small does and three swamp-hens to the other gifts that had been spared Pierre's profligate generosity. The Senegalese infantryman made a powerful impression. All the more so since he continued to make daily hunting trips and distribute the spoils. Once, he killed a hippopotamus that had been sowing terror on the river and its bank, and Malamine became Maylélé, the wily one. He inspired *respect and trust. Pierre, gaunt, filthy, ragged and barefoot, who spent much of his time in the thickets, elicited only pity. So when the poor white man offered to place all the Bateke beneath the vast sky under the protection of "his country", France, it was from Malamine's eyes that Makoko knew that he was serious. He signed the treaty. Thus, in Nkuna, was established the most precarious French garrison in all of history: a diarrhoeic Italian and two Senegalese infantrymen. Malamine appealed to an ancient sorceress to assuage the raging torrent in Pierre's bowels. She plied him with many potions, locked him in a hut and, having slipped into a long trance, predicted that the explorer would die from diarrhoea, but several years hence, in the land of his faithful companion. Reassured, Malamine had Pierre carried back to the coast in a hammock. He kept a copy of the treaty and, in the name of France, he alone held Nkuna, later known, not as Malamineville, but as Brazzaville.*

Coumba Camara
Infantryman Second Class
Assikasso

A CHAPTER ON "DEATH"

the PARISIAN's WOMAN

"Bonzour, ma coumandan."

For me alone, Sokhna reserves her first words of the day, together with a bucket of hot water which she sets in the tubs. Apart from such greetings, she rarely speaks French, though I know that she has at least the same command of the language as her husband, a Senegalese infantryman. Which in our trading post raises her to the rank of scholar. For several years now, she has shared army life with Coumba. Wherever we recruit, train and send the infantrymen, their wives go too. It is not unusual for them to play a part in battle. They are skilled at slipping between the front lines, distributing food and ammunition. In the thick of the fight, they will sometimes take up a rifle to replace a wounded or dead man. Many have fallen in battle for their husbands who have fallen for France. Sokhna is always the first to wake, Petit Malamine sleeps on, tied to her rump. While she prepares the morning meal, Coumba sounds reveille. And it is not just the men in our camp who leap from their beds. Down in the village, early risers flock to the call of the bugle.

Three infantrymen – the militiamen Djiminis, Kouadio Angaman, known as Captain Lucky, and Kassy Ntiman, who is still peeved that I have not accorded him a French first name – and I gather, ramrod straight, about the flagpole and salute the Tricolour of the Third Republic.

"Coumba, I don't have to run up the flag every morning. I'm not a soldier."

"Not true, ma coumandan. Grand-Bassam coming with much much rifles! We get may new new good guns, ma coumandan."

Whether civilian or soldier hardly matters to a Senegalese infantryman: the ordinary white man is automatically *ma capitaine*. The military stripes raising me to the rank *ma coumandan* had been mockingly awarded after several days of vomiting and a chaotic landing with the Chassepots from Châtellerault. My friends from Alsace would appreciate the compliment. As far as the little company in Grand-Bassam is concerned, I am an envoy from the sacred Ministry of War.

"Flag of France big fetish. When white man salute flag, Black man him respect France."

"The flag is not a fetish, Coumba. It is simply a symbol. A symbol is—"

"Big fetish everyone say. Sergeant Malamine him n'uncle mine long time past. He heal Congo sickness with flag of France."

There can be no discussion without examples from the adventures of his great-great uncle, Sergeant Malamine. Coumba is right about the need for my symbolic presence at the raising of the flag. It captures the imagination of a country where the most commonplace action is accompanied by complex rituals that would baffle even the most punctilious British bureaucrat. Here, the allegorical is essential, the metaphorical compulsory. I cannot even begin to imagine what goes on in the heads of the Black faithful as they watch our republican rite. To the blare of an instrument louder than a Viking horn, our little party performs strange gestures while reverently gazing at a piece of cloth with three coloured stripes hung on a bamboo stake from Guinea as it flutters in the wind. The ceremony is ridiculous, unless considered in the context of its symbolism: planted in the soil of the *patria*, the fatherland, the flagpole bears the standard, the *standhard* of shared values which men and women of the *natio*, born of common ancestors, proudly gather to hoist aloft. It takes considerable distance to rediscover the meaning of actions that, in the Carré des Invalides or the Carré Mercurial in Chambéry, were routine. We are Anyi who have lost our memory.

Coumba's bugle is not incidental to the success of our salute to the colours. His repertoire revolves around "Adjutant's Call, Reveille, To the Colours, Evening Colours" and the now famous "Have you seen Bismarck?" Every morning, he extemporises notes of his own and, when the audience reacts with a cheer or a clap, Coumba performs impromptu solos that are always perfect. He blows his instrument with such passion that, at every note, I think his lips will crack, his lungs explode. His cheeks swell so far it would put a ventriloquial frog to shame, his eyes bulge as though seeking to flee their sockets, and his jugular vein pulses like a snake along the neck. I firmly believe that Coumba's bugle can be heard far beyond the village. And he never stops until I interrupt. Here in these

African lands, from break of dawn, effective presence pummels every eardrum. Our hill has become known as Franssykro, the French village. The newest children's game is a parody of our parade. They play it using bamboos for Chassepots and a goat's horn for a bugle. The adults stand to attention. Everyone refers to me as Coumandan Dabii. Everyone except Boidy. I am still his white fetish. Morning and evening, some nephew, son, or kangah captive brings up my portion of the stews prepared by his wives. Having shared bed and board with his ancestors makes me a mouthpiece of the Boidy clan. In the eyes of all, he is head of the Coumandan Dabii clan.

Whenever Coumba and Soumaré, with Chassepots slung over their shoulders and ammunition strapped to their belts, disappear into the forest, they re-emerge like an illustration in a colonial magazine, one in front of the other, with some beast hanging by its legs from a wooden beam resting on their shoulders. Coumba is a skilled shot with the Chassepot, but since he knows nothing about the art of hunting, I doubt that his sylvan escapades make for epic tales. The jungle here teems with even more game than the forest around Grand-Bassam. In such conditions, there is no need to hunt: you simply gather. Every day, carcasses are butchered at the flagpole. For once, the blood at the foot of the flag is animal rather than human. The "war office" is a smokehouse for an endless stream of game.

Up here in Franssykro, Coumba is a major and a master of a carnivorous diplomacy in the tradition of Sergent Malamine, something that attracts even greater admiration than his bugle playing. Every day, the spoils of the hunt are wrapped in banana leaves before being dispatched to the two royal courts. His attention to detail goes so far as to deliver the meat when the sun is waning and preparations have begun for the evening meal. Whether they pledge allegiance to Yafoun or to Éhiwa, all the notable families receive a blood-smeared package seasoned with: "France does not want you to be dry-mouthed; the commandant bequeaths you the spoils of his skill!" The phrase comes from Boidy. A "dry mouth" is one so impoverished that it never tastes the fat of a piece of meat. The first part of the sentence is a promise of prosperity. The second part is more cryptic. A rifle skilled in hunting is also skilled in battle. The gift is wrapped in a promise of prosperity and a threat. Our hill, that is to say France, is not generous out of weakness; if attacked it will defend itself. It is a complete lie. In the event of a massive attack, we would not hold out half an hour, and that only because of our elevated position. But "a well-disposed bell leads to a well-disposed mind", according to Boidy. Before long, Franssykro spills forth from every mouth in Assikasso. Literally and figuratively. For travellers and caravans from the north, it is not a regular port of call. Much to the fury of the Apollonian traders, the hut that houses our Ministry of Trade is bustling with life.

* * *

The tallest man I have seen in my life is standing in front of me. He towers three heads above me. With such a stature, he is naturally forbidding. The piece of cotton that drifts from his shoulder to his feet could serve as a blanket for three sleeping people. The rosary in his left hand looks like a bracelet, though an ordinary man could use it as a lasso. Behind him, a score of porters stand in line, glistening with sweat, packages balanced on their heads. With Coumba and Captain Lucky Kouadio-Angaman, I move towards the concession to welcome the caravanserai.

"May the peace of Allah the merciful be with you. I am Sitafa, descendant of Wattara, a Bambara from Bondoukou since the time when hens learned to lay eggs, a trader from father to son since men have eaten chickens and their eggs. In the name of Allah the magnificent, my men and I salute you."

Without "raising a flag", I hasten to ask him for news of Treich. I have violated the Gospel according to Eugène Cébon. Captain Lucky Kouadio-Angaman gives me an astonished look before speaking again at length. He does not translate, he interprets. This is the Gospel according to Louis Anno, chapter 1. A bowl of water is brought. The tall Bambara empties it in one draught. Satisfied, a childlike smile flashes across the giant's face. The porters disperse to explore the compound. We sit in front of my hut, sheltered from the sun.

Sokhna races up with some kola nuts on a piece of bark, a sort of woody plate. Our host helps himself and bites into the hard, bitter kernels. Red or white and about the size of a chestnut, the kola nut turns the teeth yellow. It is said to have tonic properties. It is particularly prized in the Sudan and semi-desert lands. Among the Mandé-Dyulas, no ritual or conversation is complete without a kola nut. It is the origin of the first commercial trading between the Africa of the jungle and that of the savannah. Long before our goods and treaties, the Mandé-Dyulas had spread the word so far that they succeeded in creating Worodougou, the land of kola, in a place where there was not a single kola tree within a hundred kilometres. Our guest crunches slowly and noisily. It feels like a stratagem intended to test my patience. Sitting down, the differences in our sizes is diminished. Perhaps it is this that gives me the courage to consider grabbing his collar.

As judges of which words to speak and arbiters of those already spoken, in the midst of this myriad of languages and cultures, all colonial actions wear the raiment of the interpreter's intelligence. On their skills, their personality, depends whether words fall on deaf ears or deviously insinuate themselves. Abstract ideas and concrete plans pass through them. The role of demiurge is a precarious one. They are not saints. During any negotiation, regardless of the direction, they line their pockets behind the backs of parties white and Black. They know how to slip their interests into the murk of misunderstanding. Some accrue vast fortunes in the process. They are the first elite to be created by virtue of our presence, the leading edge of our endeavours.

I observe how Captain Lucky Kouadio Angaman adopts one stance when addressing Sitafa, and another when addressing me. When speaking to the Bambara, he is sinuous, smiling, almost laughing. Addressing the French, he is grave, upright, focused, almost stiff. Language conveys its own attitudes. At the beginning of a conversation, each party turns to the interpreter. He is the medium. As the conversation progresses, they look at each other, the interpreter is merely a whisper, he fades into the background.

195

"I am a Djatiguitchè, an official landowner. In my concession, I can host a caravan as vast as the royal entourage of Mansa Kanku Musa when he made his pilgrimage to Mecca, in the most holy lands of Allah the merciful. I it was who took in your French brothers when no-one else would have them."

"Why so?"

"Fear of the British! We knew that sooner or later they would come. Since they annihilated the armies of the Ashanti and pillaged Kumasi, everyone has feared them. The British keep their powder dry."

"We also have dry powder."

"The British are swift to anger. Their gunpowder ignites faster than yours. Especially when there is gold at stake."

"And you are not afraid of the British? Why else would you welcome a Frenchman and his troop?"

"I am no hero. I am a Wattara. I know that, at heart, the British are traders just as we are. If they should find your flag hanging out of my hut, that of the biggest trader in town, I shall simply tell them that I succumbed to your enticing offers. They will understand, and ask for details. I shall lie and exaggerate the offers of the French. They will then make counter-offers."

"Has your king accepted our flag?"

"Not only did he accept it, he personally raised it in the middle of his concession. Before a dumbfounded court, he signed the French parchment. No-one knows how Adjoumani allowed himself to be persuaded by this weak, sickly white man who had been deserted by half his porters, and was protected by only a small band of Senegalese infantrymen. It is said that your Treissy has a powerful fetish. And we fear fetishes even more than we do guns. What a deal I made when I welcomed him! My rivals were as jealous as testicles of a penis. Seeing such a lucrative deal within reach yet being unable to snatch it . . ."

And the laughter that gives the giant a child's face. More laughter followed. The audience grows.

"Yet your Treissy was ill. His belly refused to dry out. I sent him my Karamoko, my personal fetishist, but nothing helped."

"He died?"

"No, no, subhan Allah! His stomach was gone, but still he had his mind. His Anyi porters and Senegalese infantrymen, they took good care of him. Your Treissy was obsessed with two things: going to Kong and finding one of his brothers."

"And did he go?"

"Bismillah! No, not then. Adjoumani held him back, told him that he was too weak to travel. I believe Adjoumani wanted to delay as long as possible so the British would find him in Bondoukou. Adjoumani would be cleared of colluding with the enemy, and the matter would have been settled between white men. But Treissy was hard-headed. In the end, he left. He gave me many gifts, so I accompanied him to the Zanzan river, more than three days' walk away. The last time I saw Treich and his men they were doing well."

"And the other white man, did he find him?"

"Bismillah, no! But guess who was waiting in Bondoukou when I returned?"

"The white man Trich was looking for . . ."

"Allah'ko! No!"

"The British?"

"Walaye Bilaye! A great number accompanied by a

regiment of Hausa infantrymen, bloodthirsty mercenaries from the gateway to the great sands. Their rifles were long as my arm, fearsome as a hungry lioness and bright as the noon-day sun during the season of the dry, dusty easterly wind we call the harmattan. The women prematurely began the lamentations and dirges. The vultures circled triumphantly in the sky. And if I, Sitafa, son of Wattara, came very close to soiling myself, I would wager all the kola nuts in Worodougou that King Adjoumani's bubu was black and stinking."

I am not alone in being spellbound by his sense of fable. The whole concession has gathered in the courtyard. There is a shrill squeak. Petit Malamine, so rarely free of his mother's rump, is sitting alone on the sidelines.

"He takes after his father, that child."

The gale of laughter silences the child. Sitafa chooses this moment to bite into another kola nut. The hulking Bambara even shares with his neighbours and the porters. Before long, several jaws are crunching kola beneath their molars. Once crushed and drained of their juice, they are spat out. Let he who holds the spittoon run free!

"The British arrived exactly seven days after Treissy left. Their captain was called Lef . . . Lefy . . ."

"Lethbridge."

"Exactly! Allah is merciful to make mouths that can pronounce such a name. Captain whatever-you-said was whiter than a Moorish shroud. His eyes darted blue flames from pupils black as a smith's forge. He was truly fearsome. Now I understand the popular joke about the difference between the British and the French . . ."

Captain Lucky gestures, warning that the next sentence may be offensive. I nod to reassure him; I already know: it is one of the jokes our friend Wayou, the Krumen, tells to every Frenchman in Grand-Bassam whenever he feels his expert services as a boatman have been underpaid. Fourcade, his favourite target, invariably flies into a rage. He has told the same joke from Assinie to Bondoukou, and perhaps further still: "The Englishman rules over all white men. The difference between the British and the French is the difference between man and woman!" Like a migratory butterfly, nobody knows where this notion originated. Sedan is not far distant. For a long time, forts and garrisons flying the French flag in Drewin, Lahou, Dabou, Grand-Bassam, Assinie and all along the Gulf of Guinea stood empty as French soldiers went home to fight the Prussians. During their long absence, the only white troops in Africa were British. The British colonial army included many white officers and soldiers. The effect on the natives was more impressive than a typical French column of Senegalese infantrymen led by a single white officer. During the Saa Garnety War, the war against the Ashanti, Sir Garnet Wolseley – known to the natives as Saa Garnety Wossély – led a genuine British army. For the first time, a colonial power, with no troops, pitted itself against an African nation. There were none of the customary skirmishes and ambushes, but a series of great battles fought across a vast territory. Ashanti gold was at stake. The British do not spill their blood simply to see the Union Jack flutter in the breeze. Once the Ashanti were defeated, Sir Garnet *personally* led his troops during the looting of the capital, Kumasi, searching for precious jewels, royal insignias and objects of solid gold. The news of the Ashanti defeat and the sack of Kumasi shocked West Africa. At that time, the British fleet had imposed a blockade along the coast of the Gulf of Guinea. Verdier was suspected of supplying weapons and gunpowder to the Ashanti resistance. Royal Navy warships stopped and searched all European vessels before allowing them to dock. Especially in Assinie and Grand-Bassam. In the African imagination, "The Englishman rules over all white men, the French are merely women."

I am not offended. Especially now that I know how hard-working the Anyi women are.

"Inshallah! Our good King Adjoumani personally lowered the French flag he had raised a week earlier, handed it to the British captain and hurriedly signed the British treaty with a cross twice as big as the French treaty. With the contempt of a gorilla, he handed Captain whatever-you-call-him the treaty signed with Treissy."

"The contempt of a gorilla?"

"Yes, an exaggerated display of contempt. The gorilla is ugly, he does not need to scowl to show his contempt."

"What happened next?"

"The Englishman was trembling."

Another kola nut disappeared behind his yellowed teeth. He is mocking me. The contempt of the gorilla is clearly a Bondoukou speciality.

"Aminh'Allah! Since we learned to pray with our backsides facing west, we have used the Arabic script. I am Allamoko, man of God. Assafroulaye! No-one here can read the kaffir script, Allah defend us! There is no telling what made the white man tremble when he read the Frenchman's treaty. Some said it was anger, others said fear. We agreed on only one thing: Treich's fetish! Without harming a single chicken, the British turned tail the day they arrived! To make sure they did not return, we accompanied them to the Zanzan river, six days' walk. The last time we saw them, the British were in rude health."

"British fair play . . ."

The Bambara giant's eyes widen. He leans over and whispers:

"Tell me where I can find this 'fair play' fetish."

"Allamoko, man of Allah, not until you tell me, and quickly, everything that happened to the man whom Treich was seeking."

Sitafa straightens up, proud once again.

"Soun'Allah! He arrived some days after the British left. Truly, it was the season of the White Man! Those who found him sent him to me. In everyone's eyes, I became Franssitafa, the official host to all the French. He was weak and sickly and stank enough to tempt a herd of rutting goats. Like a repudiated woman, he had wandered for months among the villages of Mossi, Gourounsi and Dagomba country. Even the Lobis would not take him in. To be spurned by naked, crude, animist, infidel primitives, the man must have been truly cursed. Everyone laughed when he claimed to be a soldier in your army. I sent someone to Kong to inform Treissy. The messenger returned bearing gifts for me and a horse for the foul-smelling white man. I confess that I was glad to escort him to the Zanzan river, less than two hours' walk away. The last time I saw him, he was riding an old nag as gaunt as himself, stinking as badly as when he arrived, but your errant soldier was in rude health."

* * *

My terrace, built on a promontory, is more than merely an observation deck overlooking Assikasso. I go out there to enjoy the dawn, the one prescribed moment of peace between man and nature in the jungles of Africa. The mosquitoes are busy digesting their orgy of human blood; the furious midges known as *fourous* are numb with the dew that has settled on their wings; owls, hooting cats, all the noisy winged nocturnal creatures are silent in their trees or caves; the insects with their advanced warning systems grant themselves a little repose; the darkness of the night contorts to reveal blues still too dark to prickle the retina; from the thatched roofs of the kitchen huts below, wisps of smoke rise and contend with the blanket of fog. Every surface drips. It is so humid you can drink the air. Once you recover from the feeling of drowning, the high humidity creates an intoxicating memory of time spent in the womb. If, some day, an explorer describes Africa as the cradle of primitive humanity in a savage Eden, the thought will have come to him in such fleeting moments. Already, slender rays have begun to pierce the nebulous clouds that emanate from the earth, exuded by the plants. The sun's rays group together in clusters, through the many gaps in the jungle canopy. Passing through the suspended water is like passing through a magnifying lens. The temperature is already approaching its acme, although the sun has not yet risen above the treetops.

Just as there is almost no twilight here, so there is almost no dawn. I observe this every morning. In Assikasso, lauds is the miracle of dawn.

On one such morning, she arrives. She picks her way, one step at a time. Slowly she climbs the hill, one foot after the other. She was bound to come; she is here. I do not know what expression, what posture to adopt to greet her. I am frozen by a stabbing cold, stirred by a wave of heat. The last resistance in my body melts away. A tingle at the tip of my little toe becomes pins and needles through my leg. A bead of sweat on my brow becomes a raging torrent down my back. Our meeting has been written in stone ever since La Rochelle. She takes me in her arms, embraces me. A whirlwind sucks me into the portal of her madness. My Roman father and his last cough, my mother enveloped in a cloud of talcum powder, breaking waves of chillies, dragon factories, eviscerated cloisters, chameleon Chassepots, singing beaches, dancing horizons, pulsating Negroes, colonial demiurges, indolent hordes, enchanted forests, vampire mosquitoes, cannibal skirmishers, cauldron prince, miming interpreter, salt-flecked crocodile, carpet of crabs . . . and the tousled braids, the star-scarred belly, the flawless skin, the drinker of light, the slender legs . . . I am hers. Malarial fever has come!

Having begun as a distant murmur, the sound slowly swells, gently engulfs, until it is the only thing to be heard. This tom-tom does not have the lightness of the one I heard at Boidy's celebration. It does not just sound, it resounds. All through my head. The vibrations ripple through the ground, stirring my body. To feel them so powerfully, you have to lie flat on your back on the earth. Through the relay of bones, the ribcage amplifies the sounds that explode in my head with each blow on the stretched skins. A stabbing rhythm beneath an agonising solo. Who bids the devil come? This hellish tom-tom must be silenced. On a moonless evening, in the boys' compound, Eugène Cébon spoke of war and human sacrifice. In the earth, there are plants and spirits. The plants feed on water, the spirits on blood. To the plants, nature brings rain; to the spirits, man brings war and sacrifice. There can be no war, no sacrifice without music. Eugène Cébon knows that it is with music, too, that our armies gut each other, that we never slaughter without drums and trumpets. "Dabii, skin may come in many colours. But the spirits of all men share only one: the colour of blood." The great tom-tom stands at the frontier between these two worlds. The sound of men is borne on the wind, that of the spirits travels through the earth. I can hear its every vibration. In my head a fantasia of elephants, a ballet of whales. I am determined to stop this tom-tom. I open my eyes. I see the French flag.

Coumba has used up all the quinine. Boidy summons three fetishists, and still the succession of fevers and delirium shows no sign of abating. When my bowels open up in torrents, they lose all hope. Kassy Ntiman is the first to desert. He will never have his French name now. The Mandé-Dyula hawkers follow suit, then the Djiminis militiamen. A dead white man cannot pay. Coumba sent the Soumaré and Sall infantrymen and their families back to the coast. The Apollonian merchants thunder and rage, hinting at evil charms they have fashioned and buried beneath my hut. Every evening, Boidy is convinced that I will not make it through the night. Every day, when he comes down the hill, the people ask:

"Is the dead man dead?"

"Not yet, the dead lives still."

In the Anyi language, fainting, coma and death are the same word. So one should not kneel and pray when a dead man is resurrected, even after three days. Because of the confusion of terms, it is a common occurrence. Christianity could not have blossomed in these lands: an Anyi Jesus would have attracted no curiosity. How long does it last? They have never seen someone die so often for so long without dying. They talk of the soul of the pangolin, an animal that clings to its branch for several days after death. They also talk of a powerful counter-fetish. Beliefs waver, superstitions are shaken.

"The *coumandan* is a priest of the white religion. It is said that they killed the son of a god so as to drink his blood on the seventh day of the week."

"We all know the power of a fetish fashioned from the blood of a king's son. Imagine it with the blood of the son of a god . . ."

"Is that true? Then we are doomed."

"I sensed that his delirious dance the other night was not natural. No-one can be so disjointed, so disconnected from the rhythm, unless he is the puppet of powerful fetishes."

"In Krinjabo, they say he sleeps with Malan Alloua without ill."

"That is true? Then we are doomed."

"He slept soundly in the fetish hut where Boidy the sorcerer keeps the remains of his father and his grandfather . . ."

"You should have seen him wake up every morning with a smile on his face."

"That is true! Then we are doomed."

"Calm yourself! Our parents left us the most powerful fetishes in the world."

Assikasso has given me a kind of mystique. The Apollonian traders are no longer so smug. The last of my troop, Captain Lucky Angaman-Kouadio, Coumba, Petit Malamine and Sokhna, constantly watch me. They cannot say when, but one evening she appears among them carrying a bundle of leaves. She takes me out of the administrative hut, lays me on a mat at the foot of the flag and sends Boidy to summon the tom-tom of blood, shouting, "I am Adjo the Black, princess of Krinjabo, wife of the Parisian!"

Deluged with foul decoctions, washed with reeking potions, fed on a liquid that tastes of bile, I struggle along a road to recovery that tortures my every sense. But, a single presence, a single gesture, a single glance and the bitter empire is abolished. My recovery entirely depends on Adjo's skill in preparing her potions and her delicacy in getting me to swallow them. It is a beautiful idea that, with her hands, her eyes, her knowledge, my life begins again. Adjo takes care of everything. Even using Molière's instrument on me after the Anyi fashion. Trust. The flesh and the strength that have wasted away return gram by gram. For days, perhaps weeks, Adjo has been working to restore some semblance of my humanity that does not send children scurrying from my ghostlike figure howling, "*Saman! Saman!*"

The Legend of Interpreter Zero

In bygone days, long before we sought to establish ourselves in Africa, a young naval lieutenant called Bouet sailed the Malouin along the coasts of Half-Jack, Piquiny Bassam, Grand-Bassam and the lagoons of Bouboury. He returned to France with two things: "A Commercial Outline of the African Coast", a report intended for the chambers of commerce in Bordeaux and Marseille; and a young Black man. The report was intended to persuade politicians and private investors of the military and commercial viability of French anchor points in the Gulf of Guinea. Bouet intended the young Black man to be an interpreter who, when he went home, would teach others. But the young man was so quick of mind that he was admitted to the elite Lycée Louis-le-Grand, and excelled throughout his time there. It was four years before the French business reacted to Bouet's report; the lieutenant had a prestigious career in the navy and never again heard tell of the young Black man.

For years, Peter, the elderly king of Grand-Bassam, had been plotting to extract higher and higher rents from Europeans. He had signed a treaty with Bouet and then with his envoy Fleuriot de Langle, as well as with various officers representing the British Crown who gave him his Christian name. His kingdom moved between British, French and occasionally Dutch hands. One additional barrel of gunpowder and he would lower one flag and hoist another in its place. By adding an impressive barrel organ to the traditional rifles, gunpowder, tobacco and alcohol, Faidherbe, a particularly brilliant captain, raised the bar on what the British had offered. So, today's celebrations are in honour of the French. Brass and drums vie for dominance. Enchanted by his newest acquisition, the elderly king even essayed a few dance steps. As naked and filthy as all the others, one man in the crowd kept standing next to the captain. A child clung to his legs. Exasperated, Faidherbe asked: "What the devil does this man want?" Before an interpreter could open his mouth, the importunate man replied in perfect French: "Captain, I am a former pupil of the Lycée Louis-le-Grand. Admiral Bouet brought me to France, and the Ministre de la Marine enrolled me in the school. When I completed my studies, I was brought back here to my village. I make my living interpreting for the soldiers from the trading posts and the villages. This boy is my son. His name is Louis."

Louis Anno
Interpreter at the Résidence de France
Assinie

A CHAPTER OF
RESURRECTIONS

TREICH

"*Coumandan Dabii he dead Assikasso. Dja Kouadjo him kill him dead!*" Back in Grand-Bassam, the Soumaré and Sall infantrymen were categorical. I was dead at Assikasso, killed by Dja Kouadjo. Just as taxonomists give animals and plants a genus and species name, so the Anyi give two names to every disease. Each has a distinct character, behaviour and anthropomorphic parentage. It makes sense to give a human face to an inhuman misfortune. It makes calamity more bearable. Dja Kouadjo – malaria – is angry and deceitful. His accomplices are Nzo Guier (diarrhoea) and Vié Ngo (fever). Together, they attempt to summon their uncle Éwoulé – death.

News of my death prompted little excitement. Any European in the hinterlands of Guinea is on borrowed time. But more importantly, my death was overshadowed by a major event: Treich had succeeded! Kong and Bondoukou were French, the trading posts at Grand-Bassam and Assinie had been saved, Côte d'Ivoire was finally a colony. Treich had redrawn the borders of the French empire. If that were not

211

enough, he had found Binger, the explorer lost in the savannah, and brought him back to the coast.

In his account to me, Anno abandons the rudiments of his profession. He is not interpreting; he is recounting an adventure to a friend. I feel flattered that he slips in Anyi expressions when he knows the French term is confusing. At first, he refuses to continue on his journey to Kong. Though his diarrhoea has subsided, Treich has vomited a lot of blood. Gaunt and feeble, his every step feels like his last. Because he refuses to be carried in a hammock. "What will Kong's men think of France if I arrive in a hammock, carried by two Black men? I have not come to propose a slave treaty, but a commercial treaty between two countries." His blood is rekindled when they arrive at the Comoé. The waters are low enough for the group to ford the river.

In December, the dusty harmattan sweeps across the savannah. The miasmas of the rainy season are driven away. Treich almost seems cured. On 24 December, Christmas Eve, the meagre group arrives outside Kéwaré, where they are met by three men who are in fact Kong chiefs. Being greeted at the door, so to speak, is not an auspicious sign. The town is still a full day's walk. Led by Tano, the standard-bearer, the troop arrive in procession in time for the evening palaver. Their expedition to Indenie, Bondoukou, the British sacking of Kumasi, the robbery of the caravans . . . Treich is called upon to explain everything.

Sikasso, Kong, Bondoukou and Kumasi operate much like the Hanseatic cities. For centuries, a tacit agreement has enabled them to capture all the trade, north and south, coming in from the region. They dream of straightforward access to European goods. The British now hold Kumasi, the largest, oldest and most important town in their Hanseatic League. Why forge an alliance with the French? In his defence, Treich brandishes the treaty signed with King Adjoumani of Bondoukou, and exaggerates the presence of French troops in Sudan, where Sikasso is located. This argument hits home, but it does not win him unanimous support. The British have destroyed the Ashanti kingdom, and Kong is afraid it may suffer the same fate. Better poor trade than no trade at all. The meeting becomes even more tense at the mention of Binger. As elsewhere, the chiefs in Kong never address people directly. Here, the griot takes the role of the staff-bearer.

"Binger began by boasting of his friendship with our sworn enemy Samory: a heretic self-proclaimed Almami, a Muslim chief who leads a band of murderous fetishists. Indeed, he participated with Samory in the siege of Sikasso. Our neighbours in Tengréla wanted nothing to do with him, though they previously welcomed your father René Caillé. This man of yours arrived here hungry, sick, gaunt and stinking of hyena. There is not a white man within a thousand kilometres, yet he dared take out a piece of paper and demand that we submit to him and to your country, France! In the name of Islam, we submit only to Allah. He was spared public execution only because Karamoko Oulé Wattara persuaded the council that he was insane. He was told to head south, where he wanted to go, but he headed due north. It has been ten months since that time and we have just learned that he is due east, in Bondoukou. If, as you say, this man is your superior, that he is commander of your armies, then this meeting is concluded. We shall wait for the British. *Kouman bana."*

Like the Anyi, the Mandé-Dyulas of Kong signal frank refusal and the end of negotiations with *kouman bana*: "the word is concluded". As a rule, this is followed by the opening of hostilities. So much effort, and all in vain! Failure is harder to accept when one has come so close to the goal. With the morale of our ambassadors at an all-time low, the return journey will be long indeed. Treich alone manages to smile. He alone knows the miracle he is about to perform.

Christmas in Kéwaré

or

*How to make a Dyula Muslim reconsider
a decision taken in council*

A Comedy in Three Acts by Marcel Treich-Laplène

Act 1: Religion
Abruptly, Treich gets to his feet, turns to the east and throws his arms wide.

"Almighty God, it is Christmastide! Issa, the holy child, prophet of Islam, son of our God, is born. He is born in the land of Ibrahim, our Abraham, father of our twin faiths. This day is our most sacred day. Allow me to pray before we draw this meeting to an end."

Tano is the first to realise what is happening. He lays the standard at Treich's feet and kneels down next to him. Anno translates every word of the paternoster which Treich, with eyes closed, declaims at the top of his lungs, insisting on the last sentence: "For thine is the Kingdom, the Power and the Glory for ever and ever. Aaaaamen." A formula similar to that found in Muslim prayers. The congregation is dumbfounded.

Act 2: The Lure of Gain or Divide and Conquer
After he has prayed, Treich asks to meet with Karamoko Oulé Wattara to thank him for sparing the life of his brother, Binger. He wishes to personally present him with gifts worthy of his gratitude, "because he who gives life is a father, and he who saves life is greater than a father".

Act 3: The Fetish
Treich apologises in advance for having to broach the subject of fetishists in a devout Muslim land. He bears an important message from Krinjabo. Theatrically, he rummages through the many pockets of his colonial regalia and tosses Malan Alloua's gold pyramid into the middle of the crowd.

The next day, ambassadors are received in Kong with full honours. A horse is dispatched to Bondoukou. Despite the protests of Anno and every chief save Karamoko Oulé Wattara, Treich has insisted that his captain be present for the signing of the treaty, since he was here first. Some days later, Louis-Gustave Binger, moved to see a white man for the first time in two years, falls into Treich's arms. The others greet him, pinching their noses with their fingertips. He positively reeks.

The return is immediately planned. The troop follow the

Comoé. As they reach the densely forested area where the trek becomes more arduous, Binger suddenly falls ill. He suffers a hernia to his groin and is writhing on the ground in agony. Treich orders the last two porters to carry him in a hammock, though he himself is hardly in better shape. Anno reminds Treich of Malan Alloua's warning. "If you do not have the courage, I will do it. I will give him a swift death." Categorical refusal. Treich spends his nights caring for the patient. In the little village of Aouabo, the delegation is greeted with full honours by King Gouin Komona, a distant relative of Anno. He summons four healers to tend to Binger. Treich, wary that they might poison his companion, does not take his eyes off the occultists. As a parting gift, the chief offers us three gold nuggets as big as fists. Whether because of the gold or the remedies of the healers, Binger manages to walk for a few hours before once again collapsing into the porters' hammock. At every village where a treaty is signed, Treich introduces Binger as the head of the mission and leaves to him the honour of signing. "A man's strength is bolstered in knowing he is doing his duty, Anno," Treich explains. "But for this, he would not make it back to Grand-Bassam alive." When they arrive in Bettié, old Kwamin Bénié serves them the wine and crackers they gave him as a gift when they last passed. From here, the party travel by pirogue to Alépé, and on to Grand-Bassam. The two white men arrive utterly exhausted, particularly Treich, who, despite his illness, has come the whole way on foot. The colony is astounded by his gallantry and physical prowess. Binger's hernia vanishes as if by magic. Anno and Tano, the interpreter and standard-bearer, are as hale and hearty as when they left, though Anno regrets that he did not overcome the disagreement with his friend.

In metropolitan France, news of Binger's rescue causes a much greater stir than that of the salvaged colony. The public and the press are hungry for heroes. Since the Sedan disaster, the mayhem of the Paris Commune, and the death of Victor Hugo, the people's adulation has had no focus, other than brave General Boulanger and his beloved Marguerite. They eagerly embrace the cause of the explorer, the heroic traveller, et cetera, who, facing a myriad perils and hostility, et cetera, single-handedly traversed savage, primitive Africa, et cetera, in the name of civilisation and of France, et cetera, et cetera, et cetera. Binger, now in miraculously rude health, waxing lyrical about his solitary trek through the savannah, though silent about his trip back in a hammock, makes the headlines of every newspaper and gazette. The darling of fashionable Paris, he is heaped with honours by the Ministry for the Colonies and the Geographical Society. The public are reminded that he served as aide-de-camp to Marshal Faidherbe, the hero of a lost war and the pioneer who built the first French colonial trading post on the very shores of the lagoon where his protégé has just ended his expedition. It is symbolic. Their glorious destinies are linked. All hail Binger! Treich recovers from the blindness triggered by his fever in a hospice in Paris. He is appointed resident minister of France and has to content himself with a few official letters of congratulation. In this context, little attention is spared for the son of a peasant farmer, the boy from a rural village in the depths of France who has been given up for dead in a village in deepest darkest West Africa. Everyone forgets me, everyone except Adjo.

* * *

She sets out alone, without a second thought, without consulting anyone. Someone might demur, evoke the ancient family superstition that forbids any woman who has not given birth from crossing the River Tanoé. But what does religion matter when what is at stake is the life of the man-destiny, the man whom the diviner sees in the patterns of the cowrie shells cast on the day that she was born, the man of whom the prepubescent girl sings at moonlit gatherings, who appears to her in a dream on the night of her first menses? Man knows nothing of his woman-destiny; she must reveal herself to him. Adjo first catches a glimpse of her intended one morning on a ridge on the beach at Grand-Bassam, gazing out to sea. She spends her leisure hours gazing at the blue horizon, source of the blood that flows within her. "We are the fruit of a story that began long before us, one that does not end," her Aunt Alloua tells her. It calms her to think of her ancestors. Her family history is marked by White Skins, like her dead mother. He has come to Grand-Bassam to see them. She sees one fearlessly dive from the sandbar and, as in the tales she heard as a child, the White Skin swims to the beach where he laughs with Wayou, a man who has drowned more than one with his pirogue. Never has the beach at Grand-Bassam seen a newcomer embrace Africans with such enthusiasm. It is as though he has been reunited with family after a long absence. When she espies the rust red of his hair, her decision is made. He is her man-destiny. She is unsurprised when he is taken to Kouamékpli-kro, the village of Kouamé Kpli. The Black nation of Grand-Bassam call it Fort Verdier. When, for the first time, she penetrates his bedroom, which her uncle has sent her to clean, Adjo is drenched in her own love secretions. She removes her most intimate kerchief, folds it and hides it in a pillow. The people of Grand-Bassam claim that the woman whose likeness is printed on the kerchief is the mother of love – she who rules over the land of the most virile white men. She calls to mind Akwa Boni, mother of the Boni people, and Abra Pokou, the rebel regent. She calls to mind a time when, here, too, women ruled. Adjo entrusts her prayers to Victoria, promises her a chicken in sacrifice. Every night, he will lay his head upon her virtue and dream of her. He cannot die without knowing her. He is her man-destiny; Adjo knows this.

Our journey to Assikasso was months in the planning, requiring incalculable manpower and military resources. That same journey was made by a young girl with only a small bundle and a knife whose blade was shorter than her little finger. No water, no food, no escort, no weapons, no porters. Alone and in groups, Africans have been travelling thus for centuries. The trek from Sudan to the coast, the one which earned LG his wreath of laurels, the one which almost cost Treich his life, is one the Mandé-Dyulas pedlars make twice a year. Here, travelling is an ancient custom. Here, a stranger is asked whence he has come before being asked who he is. The kinship of routes is as important as the kinship of blood. On the journey, nature and men are replenished. Today's host may be tomorrow's traveller. Adjo's journey is in the African sense.

Adjo is an orphan, yet does not want for mothers thanks to her countless aunts, Malan Alloua chief among them. In the family, the secret knowledge of plants is passed only from aunt to niece. But the gods alone decide to whom they give the gift of healing. Those they choose are born of an exceptional collision of circumstances intelligible only to the wise. Adjo gives her first cry even as her mother Amlan Brôfouê Klaman, Amlan the beautiful white woman, breathes her last. The baby's black skin contrasts with that of her dead mother. Malan Alloua sees the signs, and takes the child under her wing. Adjo is surprisingly precocious, ever spying on her aunt and imitating her in everything. She prepares philtres and potions. Above all, she knows how to say the words of healing, without which all remedies are ineffective. In Anyi medicine, it is the soul that is tasked with healing the body. Adjo also prepares potions to thwart her aunt's enemies. Her childish fingers execute the gestures perfectly. She strives to please this woman who lavishes her with constant attention. It is for this reason that sorcerers have armies of orphan children. As she grows older, she becomes aware of the opposing aspects of her power. She no longer accompanies Malan Alloua to every ceremony – she cannot bear the brute violence of sacrifice. Matters come to a head at the death of her grandfather.

On the death of Amon-Ndouffou, whom Verdier dubbed the Louis XIV of Krinjabo, a funeral befitting his reign was held. Many hut captives were chosen to make his afterlife pleasant. The kangah are not slaves: as full members of a family, they bear no constraints or obligations and hold the same rights and duties as everyone. Many become head of the clan and sit on important councils. Yet they are not free in the European sense. They are "acquired" – as compensation for a murder or military defeat, for example, they are purchased or abducted in distant tribes. Their fates can be radically changed in circumstances that are more predictable than those of the Anyi. The death of a king is one such . . .

Surprised to see a funeral cortège in the forest where she gathers her most precious plants, Adjo recognises the woman who has been her playmate since a time before the earth could bear their childish legs. Ahou, her almost-sister, wrists bound, face streaked in tears, walks along singing the kangah lament, one of the most beautiful melodies in the Anyi world. Adjo does not have the courage to emerge from the thicket. The men brandish the multi-bladed sabre of sacrifice and their eyes blaze with the fire of the war plant. Men chew one leaf on the eve of the fighting, tuck a second into their cheeks before going into battle, and keep their jaws clenched during the hostilities. Their eyes are drained of all humanity. The war plant fires a wild bloodlust. Should the second leaf be swallowed, intentionally or by accident, the warrior's murderous madness may turn against his own. Many men have been forced to murder brothers-in-arms made insensible by the war plant. No pleas to Malan Alloua can alter Ahou's fate. She disappears for ever from the round of night dances. And with her, many other kangah. Adjo does not wait to see the funeral end before heading to Grand-Bassam to visit Kouamé Kpli, brother of Akassimadou and Alloua from another mother, who, at an early age, was exiled from the battle of succession by being "offered" as a gift to Verdier. Like a kangah.

* * *

Emptied of militias, of Senegalese infantrymen and pedlars, our hill fort in Assikasso looks just like any Anyi compound. Captain Lucky Kouadio-Angaman occupies the trading hut with Mobla, the dancer of the flying pagne who spent an evening with Boidy. My administrative office has become a doctor's surgery. Granted, it is here that, under Adjo's care, I conclude my golden convalescence. But during the day, and sometimes late into the night, men and women from Assikasso come to consult my beautiful Krinjabo herbalist. Now that the earth can bear his legs, Petit Malamine never leaves our hut. A passer-by might think he was our offspring. Boidy, with his alternating wives, is a regular guest. There is still no shortage of meat and game. Coumba has enough ammunition to clear all the forests of the Indenie. Our chief of staff keeps one rifle for each inhabitant still on the hill, including Petit Malamine and me. "Ma coumandan, you never know when the Black man him angry!" No more bugles sounding to military parades, no more passing caravanserais.

It is no coincidence that everyone in Franssykro speaks Anyi.

For weeks, the signal that will trigger our return to Grand-Bassam has been right in front of my eyes. Sokhna hints at it. "Ma coumandan not sleep at night." In Assikasso, just as back in Châtellerault, day exploits the bodies, night frees the spirits. I assume that she is referring to our long evenings spent trading worlds in stories.

"I cannot heal you of a sickness from your land. Only a

healer of your land can do so. But if you have a jungle sickness, I know ten plants that grow behind the hut. Nature is violent, my Parisian, but it is fair and balanced. Just as there are many predators where there is much prey, so too, when nature spreads abundant poison, it also multiplies its antidotes."

"Do you know any sickness from my country that has come here?"

"Yes. The Portuguessy they bring black vomit . . ."

"Yellow fever . . ."

"No, I say 'black vomit' . . ."

"We call it 'yellow fever' because it turns the eyes yellow."

"What a strange idea! Many sicknesses of stomach turn the eyes yellow . . . The Inglissy brought the fever blisters that kill children and the pustule sickness on the sex. The Hollandys brought swine fever in the feet. Before the Franssy, we did not know the nose that runs and heats the head."

"How do you treat these illnesses?"

"We cannot. Your healers must tell us how. In return, we will tell them how to heal ours. Instead of making you swallow grains that rot your teeth and your head, they need only ask us about Dja Kouadjo and we will tell them who he is and how to banish him. I have tried to tell this to the doctor in Grand-Bassam, I went through his things. He shout at me, 'Yubeech!'"

In the orange glow from the fire that has replaced the flagpole, Adjo and I tell our stories long after the hour of the Woya. In the middle of the night, these tree-dwelling mammals begin to shake the canopy with their echoing cries of "*Wo-yaa!*" Sometimes we talk until our voices fail, just before dawn.

Whatever the hour when we finally retreat to the cool earthen walls of our hut, the flames in Adjo's eyes and on her body continue to dance.

"Ma coumandan not sleep at night." Sokhna emphasises her words with a smile and a pat on her belly. I leave off my daily task of chronicling the customs of the Anyi and turn to Adjo. She is indulging in an innocent game with Petit Malamine. Her back is more arched than usual; on her belly, her navel protrudes from the centre of the star-shaped scars. A new constellation. This time out of time finds its fulfilment in that swelling. Finally, I understand. I understand Father, heading home to La Galerette, Mother by his side, abandoning his youthful dreams. When the call of posterity sounds, the salmon leave the vast ocean and, battling against the current, they return to the narrow riverbeds where they were born. Born here. Raised elsewhere. Reborn here. A carousel of generations. I also understand Abilius the Roman at the end of the Gaul campaign. He was the first salmon, the one who determined our riverbed, a tranquil arm of the River Claise in La Galerette. Going back to Abilly means first going back to Grand-Bassam. My resurrection is essential.

Our return journey belies all Treich's calculations. Tomorrow's stage depends on that achieved today, which hinges in turn on yesterday. "There is a wellspring an hour's walk from here", "There is a stream of sweet water nearby", "You will find mushrooms behind the tall Iroko tree after this river", "My aunt was married in such-and-such a village", "Do not attempt to cross the cursed forest at such-and-such a place", "You can travel by night for the next few days, a local

224

hunter shot the panther prowling..." Everything proceeds step by step. The destination is secondary, what matters is the next stage. This way, you travel lighter and more swiftly. A word of advice to all future Brazzas and Stanleys: forget those maps whose empty spaces imagination has filled with all but the most basic things: ask for directions. Even with Petit Malamine leading, our little party took half the time of any of Dejean's expeditions. It takes only a few days to reach Bettié; from there, a pirogue along the navigable stretch of the Comoé. The waters thread their deep black through a corridor of thickets so thirsty that their leaves are submerged. Boulders pink with feldspar threaten the wooden bellies of the skiffs. A few monkeys join the chorus of toucans in supplementing the clamour of a waterfall upstream. Along the banks, lines of crocodiles lie, open-mouthed, swallowing the sun's rays. In the sky, the hawks do not flick their wings but ride the columns of hot air from the brush fires. The horizon is so tenebrous it feels as though we are crossing the River Styx. At every turn, we encounter Cerberus or some other monster from Hades. In Anyi folk tales, the Comoé is always a scene of horror. Abra Pokou, the infanticidal queen, threw her son into the river as a sacrifice in order that her people might cross in safety.

Midway through the day, the turbulent river calms, the banks withdraw, the waters clear. But for the ears of hippopotami, it looks a little like the Creuse. We reach Alépé, the fiefdom of Bidaud, Treich's appointed deputy. "Dabilly!" Bidaud has never clapped eyes on me, but in the African bush, news travels faster than the traveller.

225

"When we heard you were coming downriver, we didn't believe our ears."

Bidaud is the personification of bonhomie. His tears do not stop him peppering me with questions: Assikasso, the expedition, the gold, the rubber, the treaties, my illness, my death, my resurrection . . . He has the pragmatism of all Verdier men. He gives us a tour of the compound. Everywhere, there are felled trees with "Alépé" followed by four numbers stencilled on the trunk. The La Rochelle howler tree has been felled in the Alépé forests. The company's steamers tow the timber to Grand-Bassam. Bidaud's house is built on the highest point, overlooking the village and the river. The local Akye people are shorter and slimmer than the Anyi. They constantly sound as though they are singing because their language has virtually no consonants. Determined to differentiate between the traits and languages of Black peoples, I seem to have become a Negrophile. Dejean will not like it. All of us, regardless of colour or status, are invited to dine at Bidaud's table. He likes to be surrounded by people. There is food enough to feed a regiment. "It's not every day we get to host a resurrected man!" Adjo squeezes my arm as a curly-haired mulatto adolescent appears. Bidaud has no time for the young man's pleas, he is too busy recounting the latest news from the colony. Treich is no longer deputy resident, he is resident minister of France.

"We have let the colony slip through our fingers, Dabilly. Verdier and his company are no more, there is only France. Treich has gone to the other side. Péan and his gang of carrion-feeders will devour him."

226

Tears trickle down his cheeks but his mouth never ceases its babble.

"We literally fished them out of the river. They were not very fresh. And the captain reeked to high heaven."

"The captain?"

"Not a fish, the man from Kong. By the time they got here, he was at death's door. Treich, on the other hand, was still standing on his own two feet. He made the whole journey on foot. He didn't collapse until he reached Grand-Bassam. Ah, what a sense of duty the man has!"

The olive-skinned boy approaches Bidaud, only to be rudely rebuffed. Adjo squeezes my arm.

"You know, Dabilly, I think this is the season of resurrections. No sooner did we receive the first telegrams of congratulation from France, than Captain Stinky was resurrected. It was a genuine miracle."

Even when he laughs, tears continue to stream down his cheeks. The copper-skinned boy with the curly hair mimics him, only to be hushed by Bidaud. Adjo squeezes my arm.

"I truly believe that we have been duped. Treich will not last long in this nest of mambas. I hope you're not planning to leave us for France too, Dabilly. Not the country, but that future time where every man of ambition dreams of having a street named after him . . ."

That night, as we drift off to sleep, Adjo says over and over, "Swear that you will ignore him in public!", as though it were a test of memory. In my exhausted state, I give up trying to decipher what she means. My swearing reassures her. We wake early and board the *Jules Ferry*, a steamer belonging to our

Compagnie française de Kong. It takes six hours to reach the Quai, the shore of the lagoon behind Fort Verdier, the landing point for men and products from inland.

* * *

The Krumen do not merely dominate the beach by their musculature. They build their serried huts onto the highest sand dune facing the buildings of Swanzy & Co., and it is in one of these that Adjo and I take up residence. Wayou, who shows no surprise, is quite happy to have me as an audience for his prattle. Even now that Fourcade is dead, he continues to taunt the man. The poor wretch died next to his strongbox after a bout of dysentery. "Fourcade spread caca in him whole house. Him not know swim, him drown!" He thinks that I fear I will take his place.

I am living among the Black people, and Krumen at that! The people in Fort Verdier are convinced that months of isolation in the bush have befuddled my brain. Any doubts as to my mental health are banished when I suggest to Péan that he allow Adjo to examine Treich, who has been bedridden since his return from France.

"The colonial cockroach! He has brought the colonial cockroach with him, do not let her near you!"

Dejean, his voice still as quick as his opinions. Bricard tucks the patient in. Anno is nowhere to be seen. The room is in darkness. The windows facing the lagoon are closed, those facing the sea are open. According to the doctor, the noxious miasma comes from the lagoon, while the sea breeze invigorates. Wind therapy. I can hear Treich's voice. It is very faint. I think he is calling his sister and mother. The fever. A coughing fit shakes his pale neck. Péan applies a mustard poultice.

"You know you cannot heal his illness. Only Adjo can. It is because of her that I am still alive."

"Get the hell out, you and your colonial cockroach, filthy Negro-lover! No Black woman, least of all that witch of yours, will be allowed near the resident of France. I will take care of you when I have finished with him. Now leave me to do my job."

Once again, I hear the voice that walked alongside me one night. That voice devoured by ambition and dripping with contempt. I leave. Bricard, ever self-effacing, comes out to apologise. He has received a telegram. The resident is to be repatriated to France. A warship cruising in the Gulf will make an emergency stop to pick him up. I tell Bricard again that Adjo can cure Treich if only she is given the opportunity.

I take my leave, swearing that, if needs be, I will abduct Treich in order that he may be cured. In the dead of night, having wound our way through the alleys behind the factories, the ten most muscular Krumen on the shore, Captain Lucky, Anno, Tano, Adjo and I find ourselves in front of Fort Verdier. Suddenly, some twenty armed infantrymen emerge from the darkness, their Chassepots shouldered and aimed at us. We are surrounded. Bricard talked, Péan took action. I recognise Soumaré and Sall. Coumba is not among them.

Back in our Krumenland, I cannot sleep. Adjo joins me on the beach to listen to the droning threnody of the sand-bar. The pirogues look as though they have run aground. Like a Sitafa concluding his story, I murmur: "He had a mustard poultice on his chest. The last time I saw Treich, he was not in good health."

Hoisting the sick and crippled aboard ship in a barrel in the middle of the night is an ill omen. Bricard leaves with Treich. Wayou and all the Krumen stand on the shore, waiting for the ship to weigh anchor. But several hours later, the *Macéio* still has not moved. The Krumen know what has happened. They push their boats into the surf. Every one. In the eddies off the Barre de Guinée, the whaleboats move in concentric circles around the ship. A *danse macabre*. At dawn, the news is tolled in three cannon blasts. Treich never reached the finest hospices in France. His body is lowered into Wayou's boat. Bricard went to escort a dying man; now he is escorting a dead man home. In the sun's first rays, the beach is thronged with people. I am the lone white man. None of the others dares push through the crowd. Such a concentration of weeping natives is unsettling. Bricard is first to get out of the pirogue. Dozens of hands lift the body, and it is passed from hand to hand to the stretcher. Anno is waiting. Tano too. They disassemble the flagpole that they brought back from Kong, and drape Treich with the flag. On the rue de France, the cortège heads to the White Man's cemetery on the road that leads to Nzuéti. Apollonians, Krumen, Aboures, Anyi, Akapless and even Mandé-Dyulas, all the tom-toms in Grand-Bassam vie in their cacophony to accompany the dead man's first steps in the land of shades. The resident of France is handed over to the infantrymen standing guard beneath the hastily erected straw hut, while two workmen dig the grave. Silence. Only the sandbar continues its lament in a crash of waves. A few minutes' silent prayer. Then the crowd disperses. A sudden peace. Black Grand-Bassam concludes its mourning of Treissy, leaving white Grand-Bassam to bury Treich. The report telegraphed to the lieutenant-governor in Dakar by deputy resident Doctor Octave Péan, declares that he "died, aged 29, of anaemia, consumption and fatigue".

"Monsieur le Résident, our friend: adieu!"

So ends Péan's oration. Adopting a sorrowful air, he folds the piece of paper and hands it to his neighbour Dejean. His right hand, thus freed, moves: forehead, solar plexus, left shoulder, right shoulder, the sign of the cross. Over the stretcher, over the shapeless, barely recognisable mass, swells the blue-white-red of the flag. Since dawn, six Laptots have stood guard while it lies in state beneath the straw hut. Now, they lower it into the grave. With no coffin. Moored in the lagoon across from the cemetery, the *Diamant* fires a cannon which is echoed by twelve sailors with three salvos from their Kropatcheks. The ground shakes from the blast. A clod of earth follows the body's fall. The red dust of Grand-Bassam floats above the grave. "*De profundis*" carved with a knife on the crosspiece of the wooden cross. No name, no rank, no date. Commercial agent for the Compagnie française de Kong, explorer, Chevalier de la Légion d'honneur, deputy resident and latterly resident minister of France in Côte d'Ivoire, Marcel Treich-Laplène is buried as modestly as he lived.

Several weeks after the funeral, I am in a delivery room. This sobbing hunk of flesh needs me. The black skin, the rusty curls, the line of the eyes, the nostrils, the plump cheeks, the delicate ankles, the tiny fingers ... all things from the Claise and all things from the Bia are united in her.

Land is an excuse, wealth an evasion, civilisation a fraud. Rubber, wood, coffee, ivory, gold, British pagnes, Marseille soap, eau de Cologne, Dutch gin, umbrellas, needles, braiding thread, roads, telegraphy ... All these things are but a pretext. Life alone matters. The life we lose, the life we give. What is being played out here is not us, and she is not them. Together, we must find some other name than the one that will be written in the register of the colony that was born with her.

"Parisian, Adjo should never have crossed the River Tanoé. The spirits demanded the right of way."

Pretentious Malan Alloua. The wheel of fate is greater than the carousel of our stories. Poor Malan Alloua. Adjo died in childbirth. To lose one's life while giving life is something that has happened since the dawn of time. Life, ever taciturn, jealously guards its mysteries. Prophetic Alloua. Like all Anyi proverbs, especially those declaimed in moments of misfortune, her speech carries a symbolic charge. In Comoé, Queen Abra Pokou sacrificed her child so that her people might cross the river. In Tanoé, my queen Adjo Blé sacrificed herself. Pure Malan Alloua. The time has come when fathers and mothers must sacrifice their destiny so that new times can be born and their children live. Magnificent Malan Alloua. In your name, my daughter, in the name of all those yet to come, I am much more than a *brôfouê*, a white man, much more than a commercial agent of the Compagnie française de Kong. I am an agent-emblem in the service of two coupling civilisations. One may

232

die in childbirth. To guard the child, more than a Péan or an Akassimadou, more than a Fourcade or a Sitafa, more than a Boidy or a Dejean, we need hyphens. No, Adjo, I will never ignore our child in public. You are no longer here for me to pledge it to you. Adjo, our daughter's name is Alloua-Treissy.

AN ORPHAN CHAPTER

THE LONE HOUSE
ON THE HILL

The bell-wheel clangs for the end of classes. The bell is a bare wheel rim hanging from the branch of a mango tree. The Timekeeper, a kid from year six, is appointed to beat it with an iron rod as Mikip shuts up and the televisions are turned off. At the first strike, the working-class classes shrug off proletarian discipline. There's lots of shouting and running on the road home, and games of this final break time. Raised heads are light. Most of them have no schoolbags because all their stuff is stored in pictures in the Thompson TV sets.

Just like back in De Wallen, there's a church right behind the school. It sticks its big-neck steeple right over the schoolyard under the whole wide sky. Someday I'll ask Comrade Papa why the opium of the people spies on the working classes. Émile and Geneviève's bourgeois villa of tulips is hidden under the branches of the acacia trees behind the Wasps' building. The journey is too short for me to have time to follow the birds with my eyes and my feet. So, I walk Yafoun Aléki home, then she walks me back to school, and I walk her home again, and so on and lots of forths. We take the long way down the hill from school because we have to avoid the Éhiwa house. The Yafoun and the Éhiwa have hated each other since back when they were monkeys up in the trees that they climbed down from in order to be people. At the bottom of the hill there's a mill, a simple open-air engine with a wheel for grinding manioc into a paste that you can eat. "For the Boni-Marron tribe, manioc is the plant of freedom," says Yolanda. When they escaped into the impenetrable forest far from the lands of the slavers, the starving Boni-Marrons watched the local Amazonianists. They saw them bury a bit of wood and, in a few weeks, it grew into a huge jackanda beanstalk with a big tuber-cool the locals call *manioc*. That was the name of the princess who sacrificed herself so that the cool tuber could grow. The Boni-Marrons copied what the Amazonianists were doing and they never went hungry again. Manioc made them so strong that they became mansipators, fighting to mansipate other slaves and to be free.

Before the manioc is ground, it's skinned alive. The skin is thrown away next to the mill, so on the way to Yafoun's house there's a pile of stinky rubbish that smells bad to human people but good to vultures. There's always a flock of them on the pile of manioc skins. With their long bald necks all the way down to the white bow ties of their black feather jackets, they are the biggest things to fly in the air after the bourgeois aeroplanes. The first time you see them, they're scary, but because Yafoun Aléki isn't scared, they don't scare you the second time. Behind the vultures is a path that leads up to a single house on a pointy-headed hill. Opposite is a flat-headed hill with lots of other houses including Yafoun's. When night decides it's going to fall, Yafoun and me split up halfway, because we're good friends and we wouldn't want the other one to have to walk further to get home. Here, there's no way for me to get lost, because, like Yafoun says, "In a field of hills, you're either going up or going down. If the path is flat, you're going round in circles." Yafoun Aléki is good at hills.

In the evenings, when Geneviève helps me work with my French tongue, she says it's a shame because I'll lose so many good things in the process. I tell her not to worry, that I'll never lose the mission and all the rest of it, my stead fast legiance to Comrade Papa, and the revolution and the Big Nights. Geneviève laughs with all her big beautiful teeth. Just like Yolanda. Now her house with the tulips is the only place I can talk about the revolution. She listens to me intentively. Every time my French tongue snags on a fork in the road, she stops me. I've learned amazing words like "stethoscope". She tells me that she's "flabbergasted" by my progress. Her lips look pretty when she says it. I ask her to say "flabbergasted" over and over, and every time, I laugh. And so does she. I think she's one of the hundreds of Yolandas Comrade Papa promised I'd find here. I prefer my own Yolanda. But I don't like to let on that I miss her on account of I don't want Geneviève to be unap-pointed. Click-click! The word is "disappointed". Geneviève always has a big smile on her face. Not Émile, though. I can't understand why he's sad since he gets to work all day in the chocolate trees.

One night, when I go out to the re-education camp for a pee, I hear them talking.

"Have to send him home to his grandmother, he can't stay here for ever."

"We can hardly leave him with a sick old woman, can we?"

"She's out of hospital now. You can't keep using that as an excuse. We have no right to keep him here. We're friends of his parents, that's all. His real family is over there."

"Friends are also important in a child's education."

"Not when his parents have entrusted us to send him to his grandmother."

"I know we can't keep him for ever, but at least we can prepare him. Life hasn't been easy for this kid."

"Life isn't any easier for an old woman whose daughter has upped and vanished."

"Yes, but . . ."

"Geneviève!"

"I . . . I . . ."

"He'll be alright. You're always saying how clever he is. He'll be fine."

"Bu—"

"Geneviève! Stop worrying. We'll have our own bloody baby sooner or later."

How can you be so nice and be angry at a baby? Now Geneviève is crying. The toilet chain can wait. I sound the quietest possible retreat back to my Sputnik in the outer space bedroom. Uncle's Ho's Vietcong couldn't have done it better. They can have the baby, but they can't have me.

The next day, I refuse to get into the brown-shirt Fiat 127. This time, Émile doesn't force me. We head off on foot, Geneviève takes the lead. She has travel bags under her eyes.

I don't think she's finished crying about last night's argument. We pass the manioc mill, which would have made the Boni-Marrons back in Yolanda's country very happy, then set off for the house at the top of the hill. I can't stop looking towards Yafoun. I wonder what Aléki-Joe-the-little-boom-boom does on mornings when there's no school. I see the miller cycling down to his mill that sounds like a Kolkhoz tractor. Cycling can't be easy in a place where every road is always going up and down. Not like Amsterdam. But I don't think a miller is afraid to pedal. At the top of the hill, we find the house surrounded by a bamboo stockade that's completely useless on account of there's no gate or door, so there's no point to it except to look nice. You go through a courtyard so huge it's got people buried in it, just like at Oude Kerk. In the middle, there's a grave with white stone slabs. All around there's people waiting for us. Among the people I don't know are Yafoun Aléki and her parents standing next to Éhiwa Jean and his parents. And there I was thinking they couldn't stand the sight of each other! There must be something really weird going on. Émile and Geneviève are going round giving everyone warm welcomes until some old lady appears. Suddenly every mouth is closed, every hand disappears into a pocket, every arm is folded. She comes towards me so slowly that if she was riding a bicycle in Amsterdam, she'd already have fallen off. She stops really close to me because with the thick glasses she's got weighing down her nose, she probably can't see very far. She runs her fingers through my curls, which aren't frizzy on account of the rust when I was born. She has curls like mine on her head. Apart from that, she's the opposite of me. I'm young, she's old. My skin is smooth, hers has wrinkles. My skin is a light brown, hers a dark black. Darker than Yolanda's, maybe even darker than the useless blackboards in the classrooms taught by Thomson the televisual teaching assistant. I remember Geneviève back in the fascist car, saying how she could paint my face to make me look like someone. She doesn't need to, I get it. The old lady has the same sulky look as Maman. The motion is strong, I saddle my revolutionary high horse.

"Bonjour, Camarade Nanan Alloua-Treissy."

It's not the people laughing but the smile on the old lady's face that tells me I've just talked the most beautiful French of my life. At that moment, I don't care about socialist paradise, I don't care about the revolution. I just want to see Maman and Papa. Grandma takes me in her arms. I don't cry. Neither does she. Instead of people's opium, the Boni-Marrons of the unpenetrable forests have their ancestors. When Maman left to go to Hodja's Albanianist paradise, Yolanda said I'd find her again one day; that babies know their parents long before their first cry of the sovereign people; that being born is finding your parents from a different time and a different place. After my reunion with Grandma, maybe Maman will come back soon. Here, too, people are close to their ancestors, Yafoun Aléki told me that. When you die, you're buried among the living in your house or just outside and it's your turn to become an ancestor. Except maybe Grandma. She's so old that, even if she's not dead, she's already an ancestor.

We sit down on the grave of white flagstones. On it, there's a name and a date. No cross of the opium of the people. "Maxime Dabilly – 1936". 1936, the year of the Popular

Front, the year of the long holidays, the revenge of the Paris Commune. The house on the hill is my new home. At night, when it's just the two of us in Grandma's room, with her fly-poster bed surrounded by fishing nets to protect against mosquitoes, she takes out a suitcase as old as her skin. I think there's a treasure inside, but there's nothing but pebbles and bits of paper. She brought the pebbles back from a village in France where she went looking for her ancestors. She found pebbles instead. Her Comrade Papa sent her on a mission just like mine did. She left here alone, the same way I came here alone. Her Comrade Papa lives in the Popular Front tomb. He's the one who wrote all the stories on the pieces of papers. First with his own handwriting, like Maman. Then with a typewriter. I really like stories. I'll read all the lines on the pebble-ancestors. But right now, I let Grandma tell me her stories while she spills out onto the poster bed. I teach her the sign Yolanda taught me. As I watch her watching me as she makes the sign, I know that Ogun created Grandma with far more loving room than anyone else under the whole wide sky.

GAUZ' is an Ivoirian author, journalist and screenwriter. After studying biochemistry, he moved to Paris as an undocumented student, working as a security guard before returning to the Côte d'Ivoire. His debut novel, *Standing Heavy*, was shortlisted for the International Booker Prize and won the Prix des libraires Gibert Joseph, and was followed by *Comrade Papa*, which won the 2019 Prix Éthiophile, and *Black Manoo*. GauZ' is the editor-in-chief of the satirical economic newspaper *News & co*, and has written screenplays and documentary films.

FRANK WYNNE is an award-winning writer and translator. His previous translations include works by Virginie Despentes, Javier Cercas and Michel Houellebecq. His translation of *Vernon Subutex I* was shortlisted for the Man Booker International Prize.